THE NEVERLAND RASCALS

GNOME TREE

RASCAL LAKE

THE NEVERLAND RASCALS
Vol. 1

Ted Snyder
Author, Writer

Sharon Espinosa
Writer

DREAM STAR PRODUCTIONS
Kauai, HI

THE NEVERLAND RASCALS™

DREAM STAR PRODUCTIONS
www.neverlandrascals.com
www.tedsnyder.net

Acknowledgments

I I would like to thank all of those who contributed time and talent to this book of an enchanting fantastical world of adventures based on a familiar and beloved story, bringing messages of hope and a moral sense with each new adventure.

I hope these adventures will bring out the child in all of us and stir imagination and wonderment for all ages and for generations to come.

TED SNYDER

"*The Neverland Rascals* is an enchanting and charming take on a classic theme. Inspiring and warming, it is fabulous for kids and adults alike, with a great message. A must read for all ages." —Peter Rafelson - Rafelson Media

SOMEWHERE IN NEVERLAND

THE NEVERLAND RASCALS

TAIN

Contents

Contents

Contents

Contents

Contents

JEWEL MOUNTAIN

Chapter 1

Misfits in the Snow

During particularly difficult times in old England, many children were orphaned and placed in private homes or well-established orphanages, where they were educated and cared for. Hillshire Orphanage was such an establishment, a place with good, kind owners and staff. The years had taken a toll on the old building; though some repairs had been done, aging systems had to be replaced. The cost would have been extremely dear. The worn-out roof, the tired old plumbing, and a heating system that quit working right in the middle of winter were just a few of the problems. The owners sadly realized that the overwhelming expense of refreshing the old structure was well beyond their means. Hillshire, along with the economy, had gone downhill, sadly to its end. There was no choice but to close the orphanage and find new homes for as many of the children as possible.

Most of the children were placed with benevolent families or in other institutions that met the criteria for orphaned youth. However, our story begins with the few who were not placed, possibly because they have somewhat difficult personalities that keep institutions from accepting them, or they look a little different, or perhaps their ages cause families to shy away from them. These are the few who, on a cold and snowy day, stand shivering as they watch Thomas board up the doors and windows of Hillshire Orphanage, the place they once called home.

The children were befriended by Thomas, the kindhearted man who maintained the grounds and made repairs to the orphanage as best he could. He always tried to cheer them up, even in their worst circumstances. He shared stories of Peter Pan, the boy who never grew up, and his adventures in that faraway place called Neverland. Thomas told these stories with zest, and even engaged the children in make-believe swordfights, teaching them some very creative defensive moves. A much younger Thomas had been quite handy with a sword, having learned well from the son of his past employer, an accomplished swordsman. Truth be told, Thomas would have loved being at Peter's side through all of his adventures with the children.

Now Thomas is a bit emotional at the sight of the children huddled together trying to keep warm. He turns from his work and wipes a tear from his eye. "I don't know what to do. This is awful." He worked very hard to find caring families for these children, but his efforts were without success, which saddens him deeply. As he knows all too well, they have nowhere to go now. "If I had the money, I would have taken you all in myself."

With a quivering smile and a voice of forced bravery, Puff declares, "That's okay, Thomas. You've been a good friend, and we know you did your best to help us. We'll make do. We'll just have to."

Some of the children nod their heads in agreement. Turning away from them to hide his tears, Thomas returns to the pitiful task of boarding up the windows and doors of this once fine establishment.

Hawkins starts to run toward their old home as Ambo grabs her. "I want to go home!" Hawkins cries. "Let me go home! I'm cold!"

With watery eyes Ambo gazes up and down the street, seeing nowhere to go, only snow to tromp through. "We don't have a home now. We are on our own." Those words ring in her head. We don't have a home now. It just breaks her heart—the feeling, as a kid, that no one wants you.

Chapter 2:

From Worry to Wonderment

Hawkins snuggles up to Ambo. "I'm so cold! What are we going to do?"

"Don't worry, little one. Everything will work out. We'll just stick together!"

"I know we will. My cheek is frozen to your coat." Hawkins, feeling a bit safer, peels her cheek from Ambo's overcoat. As they laugh, Hawkins' attention is drawn to the sky, where she sees a strange cloud descending. Her eyes widen in wonder.

Ambo, curious about what has captivated Hawkins, turns and looks up. "Wow! What's that?"

All of the children turn their heads skyward and stare in astonishment as the cloud grows larger and brighter and gets closer and closer, sparkling with a rainbow of colors. Then the cloud completely surrounds them. Amazed, they turn about, not knowing what to expect. They are mesmerized by the beautiful, scintillating colors surrounding them—some they have never seen before.

Tain daringly pushes his hand through the band of rainbow colors, but nothing stops its flow. "This isn't real. I don't feel anything." He swings his arm side to side and up and down. The colors just swirl around.

"Hey, stupid, not real? What do you think I am, a figment?"

Startled by the voice from above, Tain instinctively grabs at its source.

"What are you? I—I mean, who are you? Where did you come from?"

"I'm Tinker Bell, and I'm as real as it gets." She friskily darts up and down, and then hovers mid-air in front of Tain's face. All of the children burst out laughing as Tinker Bell lands right on the end of Tain's nose, making his eyes cross.

"You mean the Tinker Bell from Neverland?"

Tinker Bell backs away from Tain's nose. "Yup, the one and only." Hovering amid the children, she makes an astonishing offer: "How would you like to come with me to Neverland?"

Puff shyly steps forward. "I've heard stories of Neverland and Peter Pan. Is it real?"

Tinker Bell bolts up and back. "So I'm a figment again? Yes, it is really real! Peter Pan and Neverland and me! You're the figment! So, what do you say?"

The children huddle together to make a decision. Hawkins pops her head up from the middle of the huddle. "Is it warm in Neverland? Are there adventures like the stories? How would we get there, anyway?"

Tinker Bell's response is quick and short: "Warm enough, great adventures, and I'll see to that. What say you—stay here, or off with me?"

Whippy looks down and grabs a handful of snow. "I don't want any more of this cold! I am ready!"

As if all of one mind, the children sing out in unison, "Yes!"

Tinker Bell folds her arms across her chest and cocks one eyebrow up. "From now on, the word is BANGARANG!"

Without hesitation, Tain hollers out, "BANGARANG!"

The children look at each other and pause for a moment, perplexed, wondering what kind of a word "BANGARANG" is. Tinker Bell, rolling her fingers on one arm, waits for an answer. "Cat got your tongue? You deaf or something? Am I still a figment?" She puts her hand to her ear. "And the word is?"

The children yell out in a chorus of laughter, "BANGARANG!"

Big C, the intellectual of the group, always has questions. This time he is no different: "And how do you suppose we get there? You can fly, but so far I haven't grown any wings."

Tinker Bell once again crosses her arms and raises one eyebrow. "Just watch and learn from the figment. And don't forget THT."

Chapter 3:

The Figment Flies

As Tinker Bell soars high above their heads, Hawkins raises her hand, as if in a classroom. "What's THT mean?"

Tinker Bell sprinkles her fairy dust all over them. "Oh, it means 'Think Happy Thoughts.'"

Whippy speaks up: "Let's all think of Neverland!"

Instantly, the children are lifted up, and they instinctively start to flail their arms and legs about, as if they're swimming. Inevitably, they bump into each other, get their feet in each other's faces, and get tangled up with one another.

Hawkins grabs Ambo. "Oooo, Ambo!"

Ambo looks down at Hawkins. "Don't grab me! I'm out of control, too!"

Tinker Bell eyes the confusion. "It's okay, just THT and relax. You'll do fine. Is everyone ready? And you too, Figment?"

As they start to get more secure up there in the air, the children all yell out, "BANGARANG!"

Tinker Bell laughs. "You're getting the idea already! Then it's off to Neverland, you rascals!"

Thomas, not really sure of what's going on, turns around from down below. "Who said what about Neverland?" He catches sight of Tinker Bell flying off with the children in a cloud of fairy dust. He gasps in awe and wonder, puts his hand over his heart, and smiles broadly. "So, the stories really are true." Looking skyward, he slowly waves to the children. Some see him and wave back as they disappear into the heavens.

Thomas is still shocked by the sight of the kids flying off. "Maybe one day they will come back for me… Maybe… Oh, to be gone from all of this! There has been too much for me today. I need to go home and try to fathom it all. Tinker Bell, Neverland…all true as I hoped. Oh, my."

He makes it back to his one-room shack, where his cat, Shires, greets him with a meow. "I still can't believe it, Shires. The kids are off to Neverland. How wonderful! How wonderful if they would come back for me someday."

* * * *

Tinker Bell and the children pass through star-clusters and galaxies as they fly. Silver and blue clouds of fairy dust float gracefully in the midnight sky, awakening even the skeptic's imagination.

They fly farther and farther through this distant star-studded galaxy, where the brightest star to the right brilliantly glows. Long streams of light shine up through the clouds from a mythical destination extending into the depths of outer space. Shimmering fairy-dust-like tiny prisms energize the light with amazing arrays of colors.

Tinker Bell and her comrades descend toward Neverland and enter it as a rainbow flash bursts, extending a great, rippling, colorful wave with no sound. The children are awestruck and speechless as Tinker Bell sings:

> *Breathe in deep, fairy dust all around.*
> *You'll feel a surge as you leave the ground.*
> *High in the sky, you'll fly up and down.*

Again a surge, excitement abounds.

Passing through clouds and glowing dust,

Laughing out loud, you feel you must.

The brightest star just to the right.

Great adventures are now in sight.

The clouds mysteriously separate and dissolve, revealing glimpses of a beautiful island with lush green jungles and swamps, forests of towering trees. Beneath their graceful limbs, colorful vegetation seems to glow. Snow-capped mountains majestically tower above the sea. Sparkling blue waters reflect the beauty of the mountain range.

It is the mythical island of Neverland!

NEVERLANDING

Chapter 4

The Neverlanding

Tinker Bell points to a small cove and a quiet village nestled between the forest and the crystal-clear blue water. "Won't be long now. Our destination is just a little further ahead."

The clouds disappear. Below appears a white sandy beach surrounded by a beautiful area of large trees, spring-green grass, and flowers of colors they have never seen before. "That's it, you rascals. That is your new home."

Whippy is amazed at the sight. "I never thought anything could be so beautiful."

Okydoky agrees. "Sho' am pretty down thar."

Hawkins feels great satisfaction. "And it's warm, too!"

Tinker Bell gives the children very simple landing instructions: "That's where we land. Just follow what I do." Leading the way, she fans her wings and softly lands on the white sand. The children, of course, are at a slight disadvantage—landing is more of a challenge for them.

Aky, the first to land, hits the ground hard with both feet and stumbles forward from the impact, landing face-first into the sandy terrain. He spits sand as he gets up. "Problem is, we don't have wings!"

The others come in right behind him. Tain tries to run a few steps as he lands, then tumbles and hits the sand on his bottom. Ambo hits it, hops a few times, and lands on her hands and knees. Pinner is so skinny that, when he hits feet-first, his legs are buried halfway up to his knees.

Okydoky laughs and pokes fun at Pinner. "You all so skinny yo' feet could stick in solid rock."

Tinker Bell checks to see that all children are present and accounted for. "Okay, everyone? Then follow me."

They approach their new home cautiously while looking around. Ambo stares at the enormous tree and the beautiful flower-lined walking path leading to it. "Wow, I never knew anything could be like this."

Built into the massive branches and boughs of this amazing monkey-pod tree is a most extraordinary treehouse.

Chapter 5:

New Friends

Tinker Bell introduces the children to the locals. "That's Goatee, the goat, and his friend, Bangarangatang, the monkey, who is watching you from high in the tree."

As if that were his cue, the monkey climbs down to get a better look at the newcomers, tipping his head from side to side. Pinner looks up at the monkey and laughs. "Look at his eyes. Ha, ha, ha."

All of the other children begin to laugh as well. Tinker Bell attempts to hush their chuckles. "Don't make fun of him. He is very sensitive."

Pinner claps his hand over his mouth. "Sorry." They all hold their laughter as Pinner loudly proclaims, "He's a fine-looking monkey, isn't he?"

Bangarangatang, hearing the compliment, approaches shyly with a big Cheshire grin.

Big C, whose intellect always thinks ahead, suddenly says, "Where do we sleep? Where do we eat?"

Tinker Bell directs their attention up to the treehouse. "We sleep up there."

Crane, tall and thin with light brown hair and a large hooked nose, giggles and flaps his arms. "We may have to fly to get up there."

Tinker Bell crosses her arms and raises an eyebrow. "And, as for eating, didn't you notice the huge table? You know, the one you're sitting on."

Big C, with an embarrassed Cheshire grin of his own, slides down off the table. Tinker Bell flies up close to him and looks him straight in the eyes, making his eyes cross. "So am I still a figment?"

When Big C is about to make a profound statement, he puts his finger in the air as he backs up a step. "Hard to believe, but here we are. You most certainly are real!"

The tough little Hawkins mocks Big C's finger-gesture. "No, not just real. Tinker Bell is really real!"

Hawkins rubs her tummy. "I'm getting a little hungry."

Pinner is still looking around in amazement. "Me, too. If I don't eat soon, I'm gonna get skinny."

Okydoky, holding his tummy, laughs so hard he almost can't speak. "You is always hungry and mighty skinny awready. Any less, an' we cain't find y'all at all."

Tinker Bell plays on the hunger theme. "There's a lot to learn and digest here in your new home."

Crane is curious about the play-on words. "Where do we get...where do we go to...how do...I mean, I'm a bit hungry, too. I don't want to look like Pinner. Ha!"

Several others realize that they, too, are hungry. Big C, with his usual flair and finger in the air, says, "A tree, a table, a goat, and a monkey—I see nothing to digest."

"And you never grew wings, either!" Tinker Bell responds sarcastically.

The children are curious about everything, especially the wheres and hows of their new surroundings. Tinker Bell understands their curiosity. "Just follow me, and you'll soon understand."

Chapter 6

The Secret,
or 'I Can't Eat Bark'

The children gather to follow Tinker Bell, wondering where she will take them. To their surprise, she leads them right up to the big tree-trunk. "Here's the answer to many of your questions."

"Every tree has a trunk," Big C says, this time with a bit more sarcasm and arrogance, "but I'm not a goat. I can't eat bark."

Everyone breaks out in laughter. Tinker Bell is irritated at Big C. "When are you going to learn to shut? Your jaws are flapping when they should be clamping."

She unlocks a secret door in the tree-trunk. The door slowly lowers inside the trunk like a drawbridge. The giggling abruptly stops at the sight of a slight multi-colored glow projecting itself from inside the tree. Tinker Bell enters the trunk, motioning to the children. "Follow me, and be amazed!"

Very cautiously, they enter, one by one. Ambo and Hawkins go in last, holding hands. Ambo is awed. "Wow, Tinker Bell is right again! This is positively amazing!"

Hawkins enthusiastically agrees. "Wow, positively amazingly amazing!"

The inside of the tree is truly amazing. It harbors an unexpected very large room. Inextinguishable candles hang on the walls, casting eerie shadows as the children move about. They find a storage area with many shelves, rocks and dirt as would be found in a cave, even in the small alcoves throughout the root system. Gems in the walls cause the flickering glow of radiant colors from the candles.

A few feet down from the entrance is the most spectacular sight of all: a waterfall pouring over a large rock in the wall down into a rock bed below, creating a crystal-clear pool.

Tinker Bell realizes it's getting late and the kids haven't eaten yet. "Hey, didn't someone mention food to digest?"

Big C is still trying to grasp what's happening. "So long as it's not bark food."

Tinker Bell laughs lightly, "No, I mean real food—food. Better set the table."

The children find everything in the storage area needed for the table. When it is set, they are all anxious to eat.

Tinker Bell hovers over the table, arms crossed and eyebrow up. "Where are your manners? Weren't you ever taught to wash up before you sit to eat?"

They all jump up and scramble for the tree-trunk to wash up in the pool. They are mesmerized by the gems at the bottom, which create beautiful shimmers in the water.

While they're gone, Tinker Bell, still hovering over the table, closes her eyes and whispers, "Think happy thoughts!"

When the children emerge from the tree moments later, they can hardly believe their eyes. Blanketing the table are all of their favorite foods, along with some they have never tried before. Scrambling to sit down again, they shout and laugh, not even trying to figure out from whence this bounty came.

Tinker Bell, with a little mischief in her heart, picks up a piece of bark. "Here's a special treat just for you, Big C." Everyone laughs—even Big C.

For the moment, they eat as they never ate before, until their bellies are full and every plate is empty. They rub their tummies and stretch and yawn, ready for bed.

Tinker Bell knows how very tired the children must be by now. "I'll take care of the dishes tonight, so you can all get some sleep, but tomorrow it'll be your job."

There are no arguments as she shows them to their beds. Some snuggle into the little tents on the large monkey-pod limbs, others come to rest in the treehouse. One by one, little lights glowing in the tree go out as they settle down for the night. Sleepy voices call "Goodnight" to one another.

Okydoky's voice is heard. "G'night, Tinker Bell, ma'am. We be seeing y'all in the morning."

After a few minutes, Ambo's little voice calls softly, "Thank you, Tinker Bell. Thank you for everything."

And so ends the first day in Neverland—an unbelievable experience only the imagination could conceive.

Chapter 7

A New Day, a New Life

The next morning, the sun peeks over the horizon as the moon disappears and the children begin to rise, one by one. Tinker Bell, already up and about and busy down in the tree, is looking for something and cannot find it. Pinner and Aky are the first down out of the tree. As they approach the open tree-trunk, they can hear Tinker Bell inside: "What did I do with it? Must be here somewhere."

Aky peeks in. "Tinker Bell, is there something we can help you find?"

She doesn't answer as she pulls and shoves things hither and thither.

Ambo and Hawkins are the next ones down. Ambo approaches Pinner and Aky with Hawkins close behind. "Why are you guys sneaking and peeking in like that?"

"Tinker Bell's in there looking for something," Aky explains. "I asked if we could help, but she didn't answer."

Ambo walks around the boys and enters the tree-trunk. "'Morning, Tinker Bell. Can Hawkins and I help you?"

Tinker Bell continues to search. "Maybe, just a minute. Ah! There it is!" She pulls out a pile of fabric and drops it on the floor, "You girls know how to sew?"

Hawkins is eager to help. "Ambo's a really good sewer!"

By now everyone is awake and down in the tree-trunk. Tinker Bell turns and sees everyone present, forgetting about the cloth for now. "Well, what are you waiting for? Do you think the table will set itself? Are you all washed up for breakfast?"

The children scramble around the pool and wash up, splashing water all over each other. Then they earnestly grab dishes, mugs and utensils from the storage shelves and hurry out to the table, playing around and laughing, some pushing for the spots they want, even though there's more than enough room for everyone.

They place their tableware in front of themselves, anticipating a far better breakfast than the same old bland orphanage fare they had every day. The table remains empty.

Tinker Bell waits on a branch high above their heads to see how long it will take them to realize she is not preparing breakfast over a hot stove. No delicious smells of good food are in the air. Some of the kids get antsy, pick up their forks and knives, and bang them on the table, followed by the others. All chant, "Break-fast! Break-fast! Break-fast!"

Tinker Bell, surprised at this, leaves her perch up in the tree and hovers over the table, arms crossed and eyebrow raised once again. They notice her and simmer down, knowing by now what those gestures mean. She smiles and points at them. "Sit and shut!"

The banging stops as fast as it started, and everyone quickly hushes up, confused. Where is the food?

Before Tinker Bell can open her mouth, Big C breaks the silence in his usual finger-in-the-air fashion. He points at the table. "I see a problem here. There's no food here. I want more than imagination to eat."

In the blink of an eye Tinker Bell flies above Big C and swats him on the head. "Maybe you should have better manners and hold your tongue long enough to listen for instructions."

Everyone starts laughing as Big C fumbles for something to say.

In an instant, Tinker Bell again hovers over the table, waiting patiently for the laughter to subside. "Here's how it works in Neverland, and this is one of the best things." She looks directly at Big C and raises her voice slightly. "Now, everyone, close your eyes, think happy thoughts, and imagine what food you want to eat. Anything at all."

They all close their eyes. Big C opens one eye to peek, but nothing has changed—still no food. Tinker Bell is slightly annoyed but understanding, as none of them has ever experienced this before. She simply looks at him and nods her head. He immediately re-closes his eye. A few seconds pass. "Now open your eyes."

To the amazement of all, the table has a cornucopia of food—everything from meats to sweets.

Chapter 8

Eating My Imagination

Big C is struck with sudden humility. "This doesn't make any sense at all, but my imagination sure looks good, and I'm going to eat what I imagined."

Okydoky nods in hardy agreement. "An' I sho' am gonna eat yo' 'magination, too."

Everyone laughs and teases as they eat to their hearts' content and then some. Even Goatee and Bangarangatang feast on the delicious fare.

Big C, ready to explode after eating more than his fill, looks around for Tinker Bell. Finding her in the tree-trunk with Ambo and Hawkins, talking about sewing, he approaches them with great humility. "Guess I never did need wings, did I, Tinker Bell?"

She flies up to Big C's nose. "Nope, but you acknowledged truth. That says a lot about someone's character."

The girls chuckle and hug Big C. Tinker Bell, not able to resist the opportunity, lands on his shoulder. "Remember last night, how I did the dishes?"

Big C groans. "Oh, no, but I guess I deserve it."

Hawkins, still warm and fuzzy from the hugs, volunteers, "Ambo and I will help you. Won't we, Ambo?"

Tinker Bell laughs out loud. "Now that's what I call teamwork, and isn't that what friends are for?"

It doesn't take very long for the table to be cleared and the dishes to be washed and stacked neatly on the storage rack. Tinker Bell then gathers the children together at the table. "Look around, find where things are kept, and get familiar with your new home. If you borrow or use something, remember, everything has a place. Make sure you return it to that place. Get to know Bangarangatang and Goatee—they, too, are part of this family. Check out the forest and the pathways, but don't venture too far for now. Yes, there are dangers here in Neverland."

The children begin to explore here and there. Some of the boys head into the forest, climb high up into the trees, and look over the landscape as far as they can see. Bangarangatang tags along, making them laugh as he jumps up and down on the limbs.

Ambo and Hawkins enjoy the rope-swing. Goatee watches as they laugh and swing higher and higher. Hawkins waves to Goatee, "Don't you wish you could swing like this? It's really great!"

Goatee shakes his head, bleats a long "Baaaaaah," sits down and patiently waits. The girls jump from the swing and join Goatee. Ambo sits down next to the goat to pet him and get acquainted. Hawkins impulsively wraps her arms around the animal's neck.

Okydoky, poky-ing around, thumps a barrel standing next to the tree-trunk. He pulls the lid off and is surprised to find flour inside. Staring at it, a little confused, he thinks out loud, "Nobody doos no bakin' 'round heah, an I don't see no oven nowheres."

Tinker Bell suddenly appears in front of him. "Why are you staring at the flour?"

Okydoky thinks for a moment. "That much flour, Tinker Bell, ma'am, be makin' a whole lot o' bread loafs."

Tinker Bell jokingly agrees. "Yup, that sure am a whole heap o' flour."

Okydoky, taking the joking in stride, laughs with Tinker Bell and forgets his question with all that is going on.

After a while, some of the boys return from the forest and tell the girls how beautiful everything is. Hawkins takes Ambo by the hand. "Can we go see for ourselves? It sounds wonderful."

Chapter 9

It's Not Just a Dream

The girls walk hand-in-hand into the forest, Goatee following close behind. They come to a small clearing where the sun's rays make everything shimmer like gold. Tain is there, lying in the grass, looking up at the sky with his arms folded under his head. "This has got to be a dream. Nothing like this has ever happened to any of us before. We were so…so…barely alive, it seems. Except for Thomas's help…I wish Thomas were here with us."

The girls and Goatee sit down next to him, admiring the beauty around them. Suddenly Hawkins jumps up, reaches down, and pinches Tain really hard.

"Hey, that hurts!" Tain yells out. "Why'd you pinch me like that?"

Grinning ear to ear, Hawkins explains to Ambo. "Well, that's how you know if it's a dream or not, right, Ambo? If he feels it, he's not dreaming, right?"

Ambo stands up, laughing, as she reaches out to help Tain up. Hawkins grabs his other hand. Once on his feet, Tain ruffles Hawkins' hair. "Guess it's not a dream after all, little one. Even if it was, I'm glad you're in it, too." The three walk down the trail toward the treehouse.

The girls and Tain arrive to find Whippy, Big C, PJ's and Pinner standing with their heads cocked upward, looking at the treehouse. As the children return from their exploration one by one, they gather around the boys to see what's going on. Okydoky wanders over, looking up. "What y'all gawkin' at?"

Everyone wonders the same. "So what's up with the treehouse?" Kilowatts asks.

Whippy looks around. "Nothing, really, but we think we can improve on it."

Puff chimes in. "Especially with the woodworking and carpentry Thomas taught us."

Big C declares with his usual flare, "When we're ready, I will draw up some plans."

Everyone agrees that some improvement can be made.

* * * *

The day has faded away. The sun is setting, and it's dinnertime. The kids, getting used to their routine, go into the tree-trunk to wash up and set the table. Bangarangatang and Goatee follow. The kids find their places and wait until everyone is seated. Goatee and Bangarangatang stand by patiently, waiting for their portions.

Aky looks around. "Where's Tinker Bell? Doesn't she have to be here to help us get the food?"

She is watching and listening from high up in the tree, waiting to see if the kids remember what to do. Then Ambo jumps up. "Of course not! Just close your eyes and THT."

Hawkins adds, "Yeah, just THT."

Silently, the children close their eyes and think happy thoughts. When they open their eyes, the table is covered in delightfully delicious victuals. Crane is so glad to see that THT works he bows his head. "Thanks, Lord, for this bounty."

Tinker Bell is very pleased as she swoops down to the table. "Perfect! I am proud of you, one and all."

Chapter 10

A New Family, a New Name

Today, thinking happy thoughts, this small band of outcasts has become aware that working, playing and helping each other have brought them together as a family. Hawkins looks up at Ambo and says, "We will never be orphans again."

Ambo hugs her. "Never, ever again."

Each child hears this, and they all come together and instinctively do a group hug. "We do have a family," Tain proclaims. "The best family anyone could ask for."

They all take a moment of silence as they realize the good fortune they have had, transitioning from freezing or starving to death to an amazing life in Neverland.

The table is cleared, all evening chores are done, and the children are sleepy and ready for bed. But before settling in for the night, Tinker Bell stands in the middle of the table and calls them back. "Now that you rascals are here in… Wait, that's it!" She spins around once and points to the kids. "From now on, and always forever, you will be the Neverland Rascals!"

Excited, Tain declares, "And…the Neverland Rascals will always be our happy thoughts! We are a family."

Ambo looks down at Hawkins. "Hawkins, we really are a family. A real family."

A loud chorus of "BANGARANG!" erupts from the children.

MY HAPPY THOUGHT

I think of my mystical land,

Filled with palm trees and silver sand,

Puts a smile upon my face

With my happy thought, in my happy place.

Tinker Bell took us away

To an island very far away,

Like floating with joy and grace,

Thinking happy thoughts, in my happy place.

My happy thought, my happy thought,

The second star to the right,

My happy thought, my happy thought,

Glowing all around with tropic sunlight.

My happy thought, my happy thought.

I'm happy in rags or silks and lace,

Rainbows, fairy dust, adventures we sought

In a happy place, with my happy thought,

Thinking thoughts that I think a lot.

I think of my mystical land

Filled with palm trees and silver sand,

Puts a smile upon my face

With my happy thought, in my happy place.

Tinker Bell took us away

To an island very far away

Like floating with joy and grace,

Thinking happy thoughts, in my happy place.

My happy thought, my happy thought.

The second star to the right—

My happy thought, my happy thought

Glowing all around with tropic sunlight.

My happy thought, my happy thought.

I'm happy in rags or silks and lace,

Rainbows, fairy dust, adventures we sought

In a happy place, with my happy thought,

Thinking thoughts that I think a lot.

You'll see a smile upon my face

When I think about my happy thought.

My happy friends are a happy lot.

I really, surely love them a lot.

The Neverland Rascals are my happy thought.

Think happy thoughts,

Think happy thoughts,

Think happy thoughts.

Chapter 11

Hook's Cove

A small, quaint village nestled at the water's edge bustles with activity early in the morning as the villagers set up tables and canopies on the old wooden dock to sell their wares. Fresh fish, fruits, and homemade baked goods are laid out. Handmade baskets, hats and canes are hung along the tops of the canopies. The tables are packed with swords, guns, knives, and all other manner of goods for sale.

Pirates load ships from the dock with barrels of rum, kegs of gunpowder, cannon balls, crates of tobacco, and livestock including pigs, goats and chickens. Some ships have already weighed anchor and are sailing out of the cove. For some pirates, the work is done. Their ships are loaded and prepared to set sail on the morrow. Now, with wooden mugs of grog in their hands, they peruse the marketplace, going from booth to booth, laughing and bargaining with the vendors for the best prices.

As evening falls, remnants of the day's activity remain on the dock—a piece or two of torn netting, a half-empty flour barrel, a broken lid on the ground next to it, and some scattered tools that were left behind.

The setting sun on the horizon illuminates a pirate ship anchored in the distance. It looks very large in the water—a mysterious, menacing, foreboding figure—the Jolly Roger.

This is Hook's ship.

Chapter 12

Riding the Wind

It is morning at the treehouse now. Tinker Bell is starting her rounds, flying through the treehouse, calling out each Rascal's name. One by one they awaken, some quicker than others.

Finally they are all awake and gather around the big table. To their delight, along with bacon and eggs, they see donuts, cookies, cocoa, and milk. They talk about their adventures and laugh as they eat. Having had their fill, one by one they begin to clear the table, wash dishes and put them away.

After all of the work is done, they once again gather around the table to decide what adventure they will have today. PJ's looks around. "What is our great fun plan for today? Any suggestions?"

Silently they ponder the possibilities of what could be fun. Tain speaks up. "Why don't we start working on the treehouse?"

Crane waves his hand in disgust. "Naw, really don't want to work too much today."

Big C notices large leaves falling from the tree and floating on the wind. "I know! Let's make a big kite and fly it high up in the air. We could even ride it and fly like a bird."

Kilowatts shakes his head. "What a crazy idea. Never happen."

Big C is a bit indignant. "Humph! Think the Big C can't do it?"

Tain is curious about how Big C plans to pull this off. "Well, let's give him a try. Nothing to lose."

Whippy rubs his chin. "Okie-dokie, then. Get at it, C."

Okydoky hears his name. "Is you talkin' to me, or Big C?"

"Blimey, I'm talking to C, Oky!"

Everyone gathers around Big C as he sits down. With Whippy at his side, he begins to draw. A long while passes, and the Rascals wait as patiently as possible. Some have their elbows on the table, squishing their cheeks or holding their head in their hands.

Crane is finally tired of waiting. "Aren't you done yet, C?"

Big C holds his work out in front of him. "Actually, I just finished." He hands the paper to Whippy with great satisfaction. "Feast your eyes on this."

Whippy stands up as he looks at the paper. Holding it out away from his body, he turns it sideways, and then back again. He brings the drawing closer, holds it in front of his face, peeks over the top at everyone, hesitates for a moment, and then declares, "This just might work."

"Might work? Of course, it will work! Let's get started!"

They all look at the drawing and head in different directions to gather the needed materials. It isn't too long before they return and begin to build Big C's very large thirty-foot-wide kite. The boys tie together a framework of small but strong branches while Ambo and Hawkins sew several light blankets together to be pulled tightly over the frame. Hawkins looks up at Ambo. "That material Tinker Bell had sure came in handy."

Whippy checks over the project as the finishing touches are made on it. "Well, I think we're done."

Big C puts his finger in the air. "Not quite. We need some strong twine to launch the kite."

"Well, let's just get it!"

Puff, having found only thin string earlier, remarks, "I don't think we have anything strong enough for a kite this size."

Hawkins is frustrated. "Grrr."

Goatee recognizes the growl from a few feet away and slowly begins to walk backward, moving farther away from her. Understanding why, Whippy chuckles to himself, "Smart goat."

Chapter 13

The Trade

Everyone scouts around for strong twine, but none can be found. Crane throws his hands in the air. "Well, no twine here. Now what do we do?"

Silently, everyone tries to think of something that can be used instead. Ambo breaks the silence, jumping up: "I know! We can go to town and get it."

PJ's shakes his head. "Oh, sure! Think they'll just give it to us?"

Whippy is confident. "Of course they will! We'll sneak it!"

PJ's once again shakes his head. "Sneak it? What if we get caught?"

Big C sticks his finger in the air. "May I remind you that we don't have money or gold? Therefore, buying is not an option."

"What if we dug a gem from the wall of the room?" Tain asks loudly.

"No, that would ruin our home. It would never end there. It is too beautiful where it's at."

Ambo butts in. "I don't think we should plan on stealing anything. It's not right, and we all know that!"

Hawkins chimes in. "What about trading something for it?"

Crane nods in agreement. "Surely we can come up with something worth a spool of twine?"

Whippy squints his eyes. "In fact, why don't you and Big C start looking for a worthy trade? Then you and PJ's can take it to town and make the trade."

PJ's scoffs at the idea. "Why me? Not me! I don't want to tangle with any pirates!"

Whippy is firm. "Why not you? Besides, what pirates? You don't have to deal with any of them! You and Crane just go to the dry goods shop and make the trade."

PJ's still objects. "Oh, sure, make meee do it!"

After a while, Big C and Crane return with two very nice homemade hats, one of colored straw and a ribbon, the other of large woven leaves sporting a beautiful peacock feather. Nonetheless, PJ's still groans with the thought of going into town as Crane stares at him in impatience. "Let's just go and get it over with," Crane finally says.

Whippy is getting somewhat testy. "Get going! The sooner you go, the sooner you'll get back, and the sooner that kite'll be in the air."

Crane grabs the hats, hands one to PJ's, and motions him to come along. They put on the hats and proceed into the forest as they point and laugh at each other.

After a long walk through the forest, Crane and PJ's are finally on the road going into the town. Both look down the road to the street where most of the shops are. No pirates are in sight.

"Let's get it over with," Crane whispers. "Which shop is the dry-goods shop?"

PJ's looks down the street. "Let's just walk down the street and find it."

Crane is greatly surprised. "What? Just walk down the street? Are you crazy?"

PJ's looks him in the eye. "Yep, that's what I am."

Crane is taken aback for a moment, then laughs. "Okay, we can do this."

Seeing no one around, they start down the street on the wooden sidewalks, staying close to the buildings so they won't be noticed. After two or three shops, PJ's sees the dry-goods shop, crouches down and passes under the storefront window. Peeking inside, he whispers, "Crane, check this out."

Sitting right there on the counter is a huge ball of twine, perfect for their kite. The only problem is: two pirates are looking around in the shop.

Crane is a little nervous. "We'll have to keep out of sight and wait until they leave."

After a while, the pirates leave, talking and laughing. They stop next door to eye the display in the window. They seem to take forever just looking. Crane and PJ's peer from around the corner. One pirate looks their way, and they quickly duck back. The pirate just gives an "Mmmm" and then turns away. The pirates eventually head for the docks.

Finally, the coast is clear. Crane and PJ's enter the shop. A bell above the door rings as they enter. The shopkeeper bellows in a loud, scary voice, "What are you urchins doing in here? This is a place of business! Now get out!"

The boys are startled and speechless for a moment. PJ's musters up the bravest voice he can: "But sir, we have come here for business."

The shopkeeper glares at them. "What business could you possibly have here in my shop, with me?"

Crane slowly and cautiously approaches the man, takes off his hat, and motions to PJ's to do the same. They hold the hats out at arm's length to the shopkeeper, who snatches them out of their hands. "What matter of business are these hats?"

By now Crane and PJ's have backed up about ten feet away from him.

"Well, speak up, lads! What business?"

Crane grabs the spool of twine and holds it out. "This, sir, this twine."

PJ's pipes up timidly, "A trade sir. Those hats for this spool of twine."

The store goes silent as the man examines the hats. "So you want to trade your hats for my spool of twine. What makes you think I would make such a trade?"

Without saying a word, PJ's points to a dusty shelf above the window, where three ghastly, raggedy hats are perched, obviously for quite a long time. The shopkeeper looks up at them. "I suppose you've got a point there, and I suppose I could make the trade with you." He pauses for a moment. "A deal it is, lads. Now get out of here before someone sees you."

No sooner is the last word out of his mouth when the bell rings. The boys, thinking it might be another pirate, quickly hide behind some crates as the door opens. A woman and her young daughter enter. The girl, taken by the feathered hat in the shopkeeper's hand, runs to him and happily cries out, "What a lovely feather!"

The boys sneak out from behind the crates, out the door and into the street with the twine as the woman joins her daughter and says, "My, isn't that indeed a lovely hat. What will you take for it?"

Chapter 14

'Get Them Raggedy Rascals'

Twine in hand, Crane and PJ's cross the street and head back toward the forest. Just then, three pirates pull out their swords and knives and take after the boys.

"Get them raggedy rascals! And don't let 'em get away this time!"

Running at full speed down the street toward the forest, PJ's hollers to Crane, "Run fast! Run for your life!"

"I don't have to run fast!" Crane yells back. "Just faster than you!"

One pirate throws a knife and almost hits PJ's. Then another knife lands at PJ's feet. The boys manage to make it to the forest and vanish into it. The pirates stop at the edge, flabbergasted and furious that the boys were too quick for them. They wave their swords, throw a knife down into the ground in frustration, and threaten, "Argh! You'll not get away next time, you forest-dwelling urchins!"

The boys huff and puff all the way back to the treehouse and just about collapse on the table when they get there. Everyone hears the ruckus and gathers around them. Catching his breath, Crane tosses the spool of twine on the table. "We ran all the way! We were chased by three of the most ugly pirates we've ever seen!"

PJ's is also out of breath. "Two of them were so big and could really run fast. They stopped chasing us at the edge of the forest."

Tinker Bell hears the commotion and comes down from her little house. "So much chatter! What's the matter?"

The boys tell her all about their escape from the dry goods shop and the pirates. "That was quite brave going into town," she admits. "We're so glad you made it back safe."

All the children cheer, "BANGARANG! BANGARANG! BANGARANG!"

* * * *

Early the next morning, Sneezer, a bit skeptical of the whole kite-flying affair, says to Big C and PJ's, "You two risked your lives so we could ride the wind, but we don't know if this kite will even get off the ground."

Big C feels insulted. "Are you skeptical? Of course, it will get off the ground!"

Sneezer is aptly named because he is forever sneezing. And as surely as it is morning, his nose starts to tickle, and he lets out a loud "Ah-choo!"

Goatee, relaxing under the tree, jumps up. Another sneeze, and Goatee charges Sneezer, who tries to outrun the goat, but the animal is faster, butting him head-first into the bushes. Sneezer tumbles head over heels, grumbles, brushes himself off, and backs out of the bushes, glaring at Goatee in frustration. The goat prances away, kicking and bucking in pleasure, swinging his head side to side. The kids laugh at Sneezer as he rejoins them. Then they pat him on the back with understanding.

Whippy is examining the twine. "Nice job, boys. There's a lot of good strong twine here. Let's get at it."

Tain is checking over the kite. "We need a tail to keep it straight, and some strips of blanket should work. Maybe it's a good idea to make the center frame a bit stronger, too. After all, we have to hang on it."

Ambo agrees. "We can make a double-wrap of twine."

They finish their work and carry the kite to the field at the bottom of the hill where they like to roll down the barrels. They lay the kite on the ground as Whippy looks around for the first volunteer to ride.

Aky, ever the adrenalin junkie, jumps up and down and repeats, "I want to go first! I want to go first!"

Whippy is tired of hearing this. "Okay, okay!"

Sneezer and Kilowatts grab the two sides of the kite and lift its nose into the breeze. Aky grabs the middle. Before they can finish tying the twine to the kite, the wind catches it, and it takes off, lifting Aky high into the air. The kite goes crazy, flipping about with no control! Aky hangs from it, screaming in panic. It spins around and flips him hither and thither. Then it dives and crashes to the ground.

Everyone rushes over. Crane lifts the kite up a bit. "You okay, Aky? Are you hurt?"

After a few seconds Aky crawls out from under the huge wing, lies on his back, and brushes some loose dirt off his face. His eyes are slightly crossed. Everyone quietly awaits a response from him. Finally his shaky voice goes, "Bang...arang."

Relieved that he isn't hurt, they all laugh and help him up. Whippy examines the kite for damage. "We need to tie the middle to a tree so it can't go crazy."

Big C points his finger in the air. "I agree. This will keep it in control." They double up the twine, tie it to the center of the kite, and tie the other end to the bottom of a tree.

Aky is impatient. "Let's go again! Let's go! I'm ready!"

Puff is astounded at Aky's eagerness. "You really want to try again?"

Aky brushes the rest of the dirt off his face. "Of course! Come on!"

Pinner and Crane lift the kite up again as Aky grabs the center. This time, as the wind fills the kite, it smoothly lifts Aky off the ground. It floats in the air for a moment. As the breeze picks up, it glides much higher. Soon Aky is about fifteen feet above ground. The kite moves back-and-forth, balanced and staying upright. As it flies higher, Aky squeals with joy, "Ahoy down there! Jolly good fun, it is!"

Yes, jolly good fun for a while…for soon Aky is yelling, "Let me down! My hands are getting tired!"

"Nothing we can do!" Whippy yells back. "Can't control the wind!"

The breeze finally dies down enough for the boys to grab the tail of the kite and pull it earthward so Aky can land safely. He is wild-eyed with excitement. "That was the greatest BANGARANG adventure yet!"

Each of the children has a go at it. After the fun is over, they all agree that flying their kite was a great fun adventure for all. So much fun and excitement has made them hungry, and they decide to head home for dinner.

At the dinner table Hawkins has an idea for the kite. "Let's make a longer tail and a seat hanging from the crossbar."

"Maybe someday," says Big C, "with a lot of instruction, you could be a little Big C."

Hawkins whispers into Ambo's ear, "I don't think so."

Chapter 15

Dangers in Neverland

The children have become comfortable in their new home. By now they have a solid idea of their new surroundings and where the supplies are kept. Most importantly, they know where to find the stash of several different types of weapons. These are kept in one of the alcoves near the storage area.

Tinker Bell begins to teach the children about some of the realities of their surroundings. "As beautiful as Neverland is, there is always danger. Pirates are always looking for new galley slaves, and they especially look for children. They'll sneak up on you and carry you off to their ship without giving you a chance to fight. The most dreaded ship is the Jolly Roger, and the most feared is her Captain, James Hook."

Puff interrupts. "Oh, yes, Thomas, our friend from the orphanage, told us many stories about Hook and his pirate crew. Thomas also taught us how to fight pirates with swords. We are really very good at sword-fighting, and—"

Unimpressed, Tinker Bell folds her arms across her chest and raises one eyebrow. "Please don't interrupt me again." She continues to offer a cautionary word to the wise: "Be very careful how you think! What your friend taught you at the orphanage is no match for the cruelty of Hook. He and his crew have kidnapped and even murdered children, some just like you."

Puff realizes the seriousness of Tinker Bell's warning. "We only had wooden play swords back there. We'll have to practice with these weapons until they become part of us."

Two natives suddenly appear from behind the bushes. One of them smiles at the children and raises his hand in greeting. "Ugh!"

The other frowns and bops his comrade on the head. "Why Brown Cow always say, 'Ugh'? Him need to say, 'How'!"

Brown Cow shakes his finger from side to side in dissent. "Tall Tree say, 'How.' Me not say, 'How.' Me know 'how' already."

Tall Tree throws his hands in the air in frustration and groans, "Uuughh!"

Brown Cow is delighted to know Tall Tree got his message. "That right, 'Ugh' is 'How'."

Tall Tree stubbornly crosses his arms. "No, 'How' is 'How'."

Watching the insane argument, Tinker Bell chuckles and introduces the natives to the Neverland Rascals.

EN GARDE LITTLE MISS

Chapter 16

'Girls Can't Fight'

A fresh voice is suddenly heard from a branch above the table: "So, Tinker Bell,

who are the newcomers?"

"These are the Neverland Rascals."

"Good name. Neverland Rascals it is!"

It is Peter Pan, with his hands on his hips.

Tinker Bell instantly flies up to greet him. "Thanks, Peter. Thought you'd like that name as much as I do." Then she flies back down to the curious children. "Hey, wake up! Surely you know who this is?"

After a moment, Peter follows Tinker Bell out from under the branch and hovers with her in front of the kids, whose mouths are agape as they stare in amazement at the youthful figure clad in green.

Pinner is the first to shake it off. "Why, yes, of course—it's Peter Pan!"

Peter gets right down to the business at hand. "Tinker Bell, we have a serious problem. Hook has captured all the kids. They're being held on the Jolly Roger. I'll need your help to get them back." He points to Tall Tree and Brown Cow. "And yours, too!"

Peter and Tinker Bell begin to collect weapons and place them on the table. Peter stops abruptly, noticing that the Rascals haven't moved from their spots. "Well, don't just sit there! Make yourselves useful! After all, I have to get the kids back, you know."

Tinker Bell adds, "I was wondering where they were, but I didn't know where to find you. Now Hook has them!"

Peter reassures her, "We'll get 'em back!"

Hawkins jumps forward, gung-ho for action. "We'll help you fight the pirates, and I'll rip their lip!"

Peter smiles smugly, his arms akimbo. "But you're a girl! Girls can't fight! They're…well…girls!"

Ambo, offended by Peter's statement, grabs a sword. In an instant she's in Peter's face, forcing him to step back. "Oh, really? Well just try me!"

Peter grins. "Maybe I won't have to rescue them by myself after all. En garde, little miss!" Tain points at Ambo. "Watch this, Big C!"

Ambo raises her sword in very good form and accepts Peter's challenge. They parry on the ground, up on the table, down again, and behind the tree. Pushing Peter back a few steps, Ambo remembers Thomas' lessons and fights on with spunk.

"Watch out for Goatee!" Tinker Bell warns Peter—but too late. He backs up right into the goat and tumbles backward over him.

Ambo moves in for the sting. "So girls can't fight?"

Peter laughs heartily. "Okay, okay! Glad you're on our side!"

Tinker Bell, surprised, laughs as well. "Lessons by Thomas! Not bad!"

Everyone laughingly cheers, "BANGARANG!" Tain winks at Big C.

The table is now replete with all sorts of fighting gear—swords, knives, slingshots, ropes, nets, other sharp pointy things, and more. As evening falls, they all gather round and listen intently as Peter explains his plan.

"And that's how we'll do it," he concludes. "Now get some sleep. We'll be on our way very early on the morrow."

Chapter 17

The Plan to Get Caught?

Very early the next morning, while the pirate crew still sleeps, Peter Pan and Tinker Bell quietly fly down and board the Jolly Roger. They locate the ship's armory and gather as many weapons as there are kids. Peter grabs the keys hanging outside the hold where the kids are imprisoned and unlocks the door. Tinker Bell distributes the weapons among the kids as Peter tells them the plan and what they are to do. Remaining in the hold, they wait quietly for the signal as Peter and Tinker Bell hide in the shadows on deck for just the right moment.

Meanwhile, the Rascals are on the dock, pretending to check out the wares, hoping Hook's men will see them, capture them and take them aboard the Jolly Roger. Four pirates slowly creep in, draw their swords and surround the Rascals. One particularly mean-looking red-bearded pirate, aptly named "The Red," snarls, "'Aven't seen yer bunch round here before. Yer bunch be too small for bein' a pirate, so's we just be callin' yer Pi-rites. Now we'll get real acquainted, harr."

The pirates laugh as they nudge the kids further down the dock. One of them points to the kids. "Pi-rites! That thar is funny, mate!"

Puff, pretending to cower, points to Hook's ship at anchor in the cove. "Oh, please, you're not going to take us to…to that ship, are you?"

The pirates laugh again as The Red tries to intimidate the Rascals. "Aargggh, good idea! We'll take you straight away to Cap'n Hook!" The pirates herd the children to the dinghies at the end of the dock and push and shove them into the little boats.

"You can row, can't you, little pirites?" bellows another pirate. "Now get to it! We 'aven't all day."

As the dinghies approach the ship, there is some unusual splashing in the water, but no one notices it. The Red proudly announces, "Look at what we got 'ere! A gift for the Cap'n." He turns toward the Rascals. "You'll make a fine gift for 'im, all right."

A sleepy voice comes from up on the ship's deck: "Not another lot of those dratted urchins? More mouths to feed."

The pirates shove the children up the rope ladder and onto to the deck. The water splashes again. A crocodile appears for a moment, and only one of the Rascals notices it. Hook comes out of his cabin to see what is causing the ruckus.

The sleepy voice speaks again, "More of these filthy little urchins. They better have strong backs."

At this very moment, when Hook is least expecting it, Peter gives the signal. The imprisoned kids who are armed with the pirate's own weapons begin the skirmish, and Tinker Bell appears on deck with Peter. The Rascals scramble to pick up their weapons from the place where Peter hid them and join the kids in fighting the pirates. Thankfully, not too many pirates are on board. Back and forth they fight. This pirate and that pirate fall to the deck, dead. Some of the children are injured but fight on. Soon all of the kids have subdued the pirate crew.

Ambo winks at Hawkins. "Thomas's lessons!"

Some of the Neverland Rascals are still fighting with Hook, but he manages to keep them at bay. Tain jumps toward Hook and then back. Each Rascal jumps and moves so fast and so much Hook doesn't know where to turn next.

Pinner sticks Hook in the leg. Hook swipes at Pinner, who ducks. Whippy stabs Hook in the rear with his sword and makes Hook jump. He spins around, only to find Whippy too far back to get back at him. Tain sticks Hook in the rear again, making him holler and spin around, yelling, "Arrrgh, you lowly bottom feeders! Stand and fight like a man!"

"But we're children, ha!" Tain yells back.

Peter jumps into the fray. "This one's mine, kids, all mine!"

Peter and Hook lunge at each other with their swords. One moment Hook has the upper hand: "Prepare to die once and for all, green boy!"

But in an instant, Peter gets the upper hand. He lunges and thrusts his sword at Hook until he drops his sword and is defenseless. "Oh, no, not this easy, Hook! Pick it up and die like a man!"

Hook twirls around and grabs his sword to face Peter again. The fight continues for several minutes until at last Hook is at the ship's side rail. Peter has the advantage he was looking for.

"Bad form!" Hook jeers. Peter lunges at him, forcing him to jump overboard, not knowing the croc awaits. Thus perishes James Hook…or so it would have seemed.

Chapter 18:

Smee the Brave

Smee, who has been watching the melée from Hook's cabin door, waits until he sees Peter and the kids leave the ship. Warily, he sneaks out and makes his way to the spot where Hook jumped into the sea. Climbing up and looking down, he sees the enormous crocodile as it slowly swims away through the water below.

A sudden, fierce, fearless bravery overtakes Smee. Without a thought he yells to the remaining pirate crew, "Man the dinghies!" The small boats drop from the ship and immediately chase after the croc until they surround the giant creature.

Smee yells out, "Net and gaff the dangerous creature!"

Realizing it is surrounded, the croc thrashes its tail, hits one of the pirates and knocks him out of the boat, but just as quick he is back in. The croc charges another boat as another pirate throws a net around its tail and stops it. It gives a whip of its tail, which causes an enormous wave and nearly sinks a boat. One pirate, then another, throws nets on the creature as it twists and rolls, tightening the nets even more. One pirate's hand is caught in the net, and he is yanked overboard. Two others grab him and pull him free.

Once the crocodile is captured in the nets, Smee orders the men to kill the monster and drag it back to the dock. "Get a good hold on 'er, mateys! Bash 'er 'ead in! Don't let 'im get away!"

The crew summarily stab and bash at the croc until it lays immobile in the nets. It is finished. The great creature is dead. As they drag the carcass back toward the dock, the pirates began to sing:

> *Oh, What a Croc*
>
> *A big ole croc is history,*
>
> *No need to worry or flee.*
>
> *There'll be no more tick-tock*
>
> *Dragging 'im to the dock.*
>
> *Oh, heave-ho,*
>
> *Oh, what a croc!*
>
> *I've been a pirate all of my life.*
>
> *I bore a musket, and a long knife.*
>
> *There'll be no more talk*
>
> *'Bout Hook gettin' caught,*
>
> *Draggin' the croc to the dock.*
>
> *Just want good words, you understand,*
>
> *Memories of Hook in Neverland,*
>
> *Draggin' the croc to the dock.*
>
> *Oh, heave-ho,*
>
> *Oh, what a croc!*
>
> *Never again following our ship.*
>
> *Who brings up that will take a dip.*
>
> *I give ye fair warning,*
>
> *The chatter will stop,*

But oh, heave-ho,

Oh, what a croc!

Strike up the main sail, it's a new day!

The captain we knew has fallen prey!

That monster is gone, no more alarm clock!

Oh, heave-ho,

Oh, what a croc!

As they reach the dock, Smee orders the men to hoist the giant carcass up onto the dock and lay it out for all to see. "We'll honor Hook by laying the dead beast out to dry up—a fittin' reminder of our Cap'n."

A crowd gathers around the croc lying motionless on the dock as Smee stands with one foot up on the beast's body and boasts the news:

"This croc on the dock

Is the croc that ate the clock

And the hand of Hook—

The same evil croc

That for years Hook was stalked.

Now the croc 'as finished 'im off

And made Hook its final meal,

This giant beast on the dock."

A curious pirate in the crowd asks, "Are you sayin' Hook is dead inside the croc? How do you know?"

Smee points to his eyes. "I seen it with me own two eyes, and I killed it!

I killed it for doin' in the Cap'n! I'm the one who killed the beast. I'm the one who honors Hook. Let it lay here and dry up and be a reminder to all who see it!" With that Smee climbs into one of the dinghies and rows out to re-board the Jolly Roger, where he goes directly to Hook's cabin.

Some pirates silently pass by the now-fallen beast, a tribute to the fearless, terrible Captain James Hook. Two drunken pirates stop and gaze at it. One shakes his head. "I can't believe that this dead old croc brought Hook to his end."

"Aye," says the second, "right as Hook and the Pan were fighting to the end, Hook just jumped over and disappeared into its mouth."

"Just ate Cap'n Hook, just like that."

Chapter 19

Hookless in Neverland, or Tales from a Tavern

Night falls upon the village as the moon and stars fill the sky. A bell tolls the hour as the watchman lights lanterns down the dock. All is quiet there, except for the four causing a disturbance at one end and the whispers of two others, Sparky and Jenks, at the other near a wooden flour barrel by the croc.

Sparky speaks in a low monotone. "No Hook? We're doomed."

Jenks just shakes his head. "Negative, negative! You're always so negative."

The commotion of the pirates at the other end diverts Sparky's attention. Two of them are engaged in a fracas as a midget with a bandana on his head and a tall, thin, wiry looking fellow watch them. As the argument heats up, the two bystanders appear to whisper to each other. Silently, the midget sneaks up, unnoticed, behind the arguing pirate. With one quick movement and a very sharp knife he cuts the money pouch hanging from the pirate's waistband. The two run down the dock and disappear into the darkness to split the booty.

Sparky, who has observed the whole incident, shakes his head and sadly mutters, "We're all doomed."

Jenks frowns with his big, bushy unibrow and rolls his eyes. Heedless of his surroundings, he turns to walk away, tripping over his own foot. In an attempt to regain his balance he trips again. Arms and legs fly all over as he topples and lands head-first into a wooden barrel. Trying to get out, he rocks the barrel. It teeters and falls over. Jenks and barrel roll down two steps as it spills flour all along the way. He frees himself by crawling backwards out of the barrel. He stands up and brushes off his clothes and face, leaving his unibrow and hair white with flour. Grunting and baring his snaggly teeth, he glares at the barrel, kicks it, and then stomps away with a trail of flour spilling from his hair.

Sparky shakes his head in pity. With a low "Uuurrr" he walks away.

* * * *

Just before the tree-line of the forest is a small quaint tavern. A row of windows line the front of it. The floor is old and built of dirty, worn planks. It has just room enough for twenty-five guests and the small band of three pirate musicians. A lively pirate with reddish hair and beard plays a squeezebox-type accordion. A skinny, energetic six-foot-six pirate with black hair and beard plunks on a bucket-bass. A very plump, happy-go-lucky pirate strums an old English-type guitar. One bartender and one barmaid are present.

Jenks and Sparky are having dinner at the tavern. As they eat, Jenks does most of the talking. He has a bad habit of talking with his mouth full and dropping food and sometimes spraying Sparky with pieces that fly from his mouth as he talks. "So, Sparky," as he spits food with the 'Sp' of Sparky's name, "do you think Smee will become Cap'n? Who else could? No one I know!"

Sparky just grunts and keeps eating.

"You know, Sparky"—again he spits food, which this time hits Sparky's nose and sticks to it—"Smee isn't as smart as Hook was, but he does know a lot." Jenks pauses, then raises one hand in the air and declares, "Maybe I should be Cap'n! Argh!"

Sparky stops eating and wipes off his nose. He looks up at Jenks, shakes his head in disgust, and groans, "Uuuuuurrrr."

Jenks notices a wench dancing around the tavern to the pirate song the band plays. He watches her dance and twirl around the tables and bar. He raises his unibrow in pleasure as he taps his fork to the beat of the music. As she dances closer to their table, he gets so excited that food cascades from his mouth and his fork falls to the floor.

Sparky shakes his head again and groans, "Uuuuh."

While Jenks is under the table retrieving his fork, the barmaid approaches the table to deliver more tankards of ale. At that moment Jenks gets up, and his head collides with her tray, tipping it and drenching the wench with ale. She cries out and backs away. "You halfwit!"

Jenks unsteadily stands to his feet, apologizing profusely and attempting to offer help. He reaches out with a napkin, but in doing so he trips over his own foot and flies headlong into her wet dress, knocking her down to the floor and landing on top of her.

He tries to lift himself off of her as she struggles to get out from under him. Finally, with all of the energy she can muster, she shoves him, causing him to roll off to the side and leaving them sitting on the floor, staring at each other.

"Sorry, miss! I'm sorry!"

"You're sorry? You're sorry, all right! What did you think you were doing?"

Jenks is stunned. The barmaid continues her tirade as she stands up and puts her hands on her hips. "That's the problem! You don't think! You think you think, but you don't think!"

Still on the floor, Jenks stares up at her with a goofy, sheepish, snaggle-toothed smile. She calls the bartender over. "I don't know why they keep letting them in here!"

The bartender throws down his towel, walks over to Jenks, and with one hand grabs him by the back of the shirt, stands him up on his feet, snatches Sparky in his other hand, and drags both of them to the door. With one big toss the two are flying out onto the street, tumbling and landing on their bottoms, inciting laughter from pirates passing by.

Jenks brushes himself off, gets up, and gazes back at the tavern door with a glare and a grunt. Then he looks back over at Sparky with a double blink. "I tell ya, Sparky, I almost got done eating before we got the shove this time, and we didn't have to pay."

Sparky just shakes his head and walks down the street in disgust. Jenks starts to follow but steps on his own foot, trips and hits the ground with a thud. Sparky turns in time to see Jenks jump up with a sheepish grin as if nothing happened. Sparky turns back and keeps walking with a grimace on his face. Jenks catches up, and they head down a dirt street toward the dock, passing a few pirates here and there. Flickering street lanterns cast a soft yellow glow, lighting their way.

Back in the tavern the barmaid cleans the tables and talks to the bartender. "How did Hook ever put up with those two? I have never seen two pirates so dumb."

"Dumb and ugly," the bartender agrees.

She places a few empty mugs on the bar and wipes her hands on her apron as she heads for another table. She suddenly turns back to the bartender with a serious, contemplative look. "What do you think will happen now that Hook is gone?"

The bartender shrugs his shoulders. "Don't know." He scratches his head. "I just don't know. Things are already getting out of hand in Neverland."

Just then two pirates start to fight. The band stops playing, and the other pirates enthusiastically cheer them on. The barmaid throws up her hands and groans, "Not another fight."

The bartender breaks up the fight and throws the pirates out. As he returns he replies, "See what I mean? I just don't know."

Chapter 20

Treehouse Celebration

The treehouse is alive with activity. A party to celebrate the demise of Hook is in progress. A twenty-foot-long wooden table with benches is filled with table lights and decorations around mugs of cocoa and cakes. Some of the boys sit at the table while others stand about, all enjoying the festivities. Tinker Bell celebrates by constantly flying in, out and over the activities and looping through the kids at play.

Sneezer sits on the table with his feet on the bench. He feels a sneeze coming on. Tain grabs a cloth to cover Sneezer's face. "Oh, no, you're not doing that now."

Sneezer sneezes into the cloth, which muffles his explosion. Goatee, who has been sleeping right nearby, lifts his head as if he has heard something. Looking around, he doesn't seem to hear it anymore, so he lays his head back down.

Tain wraps the cloth around Sneezer's face and ties it in the back like a bandit's mask. "That should do it." Tain laughs.

Puff appears in worn knee-length pants and a long puffy sleeved shirt under a vest. He jumps atop the table, raising an old wooden mug in one hand and placing the other hand on his hip. "Gather 'round for a toast! How much better can it get? We're in Neverland, and no Hook!"

He lifts his mug higher in the air and shouts, "BANGARANG!" three times, and everyone echoes his cry each time. Then, in unison, they all shout, "BANGARANG, BANGARANG, BANGARANG!"

Big C is wearing thick, black-rimmed glasses, and his dark hair is combed straight down. He jumps up on the table and does a dance as Crane jumps up next to Puff and Big C high-jumps in the air. The others come close and watch the boys as they begin to play-act on the table.

Puff grabs his sword, points it at Crane, and says in a low voice, "I am Hook."

Crane lifts his sword into the air. "I am Peter Pan."

They fence down to the other end of the table, where Puff jumps off and Crane follows. Soon Crane has Puff pinned up against the tree. "This is your end, Hook!" He pretends to kill Puff, who acts as if he is dying and falls to one knee. Leaning on his sword and coughing, he whispers loudly, "No, it can't be! I am Neverland, nooooo!"

All of the boys start marching around the table in single-file, cheering and chanting, "Hook is dead! Hook is dead!"

"The croc is fed, and Hook is dead!" adds Whippy.

A loud "BANGARANG!" is yelled out.

Tinker Bell joins in and flies along with the boys as they continue to celebrate Hook's demise. Off to the side, Ambo and Hawkins laugh and dance around with their arms locked together.

THE GNOME TREE

Chapter 21

Give the Croc's Butt a Boot

A surreal lighting effect created by the full moon and a nearby lantern illuminate the crocodile. In the silence of the night you can hear the muffled ticking of a clock emanating from it, followed by a sloshing sound and a slight movement, almost as if the croc were coming back to life.

After a moment, more noise comes from the croc's tail end. It starts to move some and then stops. Silence… Then crunching and soft thud noises can be heard coming from inside the croc. Does the croc still live? All at once a big black boot pushes through its butt-end. The shiny buckle catches the moonlight.

The huge silvery moon silhouettes the Jolly Roger against the night sky while the soft light of many lanterns aboard glows through a blue haze. The muffled sound of pirates singing in the distance is mingled with the sound of rowboat oars striking the water. As the boat nears the ship, the oars stop sloshing. A small thud of wood on wood leaves only the muted sound of the pirates' singing.

Though unseen, the bright moonlight catches the flash of shiny metal. The rope ladder bangs against the side of the ship. A silhouette against the moon reaches up to the railing and onto the ship. The shadowy figure quickly disappears.

Chapter 22

Smee's Hand Full of Treasure

Below the deck is a porthole. A yellow flickering light catches the movement of someone inside. It is Smee, seated at Hook's desk, holding handfuls of treasure to his face, as if smelling it. Booty covers the desk. The light from the hanging lantern twinkles as it reflects off the shiny gold in the pile, like stars in the sky. Smee rises from the chair and dances around the desk, sweeping up handfuls of the loot, listening to it jingle when falling back into the pile. Then he sings a pirate song:

Hands Full of Treasure

I'm feelin' it, enjoyin' it,

I'm lovin' it, my friend.

I pick it up, I stack it up,

Clear up to my chin.

Hands full of treasure,

Hands full of treasure,

Hands full of treasure

Be pleasure to Smee.

Hands full of treasure,

Hands full of treasure,

Hands full of treasure

Be pleasure to Smee.

The sound of it, the look of it,

A piece of it, I smile.

The sight of it, the thought of it,

It just drives me wild.

Hands full of treasure,

Hands full of treasure,

Hands full of treasure

Be pleasure to Smee.

Hands full of treasure,

Hands full of treasure,

Hands full of treasure

Be pleasure to Smee.

Pirates dreams of such a gleam,

Fingers run through the pile

I start to sing, I find a ring,

I laugh, dance, and smile.

Hands full of treasure,

Hands full of treasure,

Hands full of treasure

Be pleasure to Smee.

Hands full of treasure,

Hands full of treasure,

Hands full of treasure

Be pleasure to Smee.

> *I can't bear the glitter there,*
> *Haargh! What a find!*
> *A desk full, a pocket full,*
> *A chest full be mine.*

Smee abruptly stops dancing and singing. His eyes widen, and his lips quiver. "Wait! What's to happen to me! What do I do? Where will I go? What will happen to Neverland without Hook?" He is very still for a moment, and then he looks up, rubbing his chin. Slowly, a big grin forms on his face as he begins to softly chant:

> *Aye, maybe Ieee,*
> *Ieee can be Cap'n!*
> *Captain Smee, Captain Smee.*
> *I'll run Neverland, Captain Smee,*
> *That's me, I am he, Captain Smee!"*

Once again he begins to dance, making his way back to the desk, where he picks up handfuls of treasure, eyes the gold lovingly, and holds it against his cheek. Just as quickly, he lowers his hand, his eyes shift from side to side, and his facial expression turns suspicious.

The moonlight shining into the cabin through the small window behind him reveals a blurred figure of someone in front of the window. Smee, with his back still to the window, looks at the gold again. An evil smile once more appears on his face.

Chapter 23

"Hello, Smee"

The figure behind Smee moves toward him, and Smee senses a presence. Slowly, and a bit apprehensively, he turns around to a quickly advancing figure and is startled out of his wits. His eyebrows shoot up, and he screeches like a little girl as he jumps back, bumping into the desk and flipping upside-down over the desk and onto the floor.

After a few seconds he grasps the top of the desk with sweaty palms and pulls himself up. First, his eyebrows show, as if resting on the edge of the desk. His eyes are barely peeking over. Then, like a flash of lightning, he is face to face with the figure. The glow of a candle shines on the figure's face, giving him a ghostly aura.

"Hello, Smee."

Smee jerks back, terrified, as if he had indeed seen a ghost. "Hook? It's Hook! Me eyes lie to me! A ghost you are!" He points at the dark figure. "Stay back now! Stay back!"

He rubs his eyes and looks again; Hook is still there. Smee carefully takes a closer look. "But how? When? You were, we saw—" He gulps a big breath and stares in silent disbelief, then finally realizes it truly is Hook. With shaky legs, Smee stands up, cracks a big smile and spreads his arms. "Hoooook, you're back!" He happily starts dancing and singing, "Hook is back! Hook is back!

La, la, la, la, la!"

It is a catchy tune, and Hook twists his hook in time to Smee's song. Hook, dirty and messy from his ordeal, gives a big toothy smile. "Ha, ha, ha. Yes, Smee, it is me."

Smee chatters with excitement. "Everyone will be…they all must…I'll tell 'em all! Yes, that's it! I'll tell all of Neverland that Hook is back!" He excitedly heads for the door. Hook, who is no longer laughing, reaches out his hook and snags Smee's collar, throwing him off-balance. He dances backwards as Hook pulls him close.

"You'll tell no one! No one must know—not until the time is right. I must leave for a while. It may be a long while. I'll return quietly in the night when the time is right. You hold down the ship until then, Smee."

Smee, a little sad the Captain is leaving so soon, doesn't know why or where he'll be, but gives him a salute. "I'll do 'er, Cap'n."

*　*　*　*

Back at the treehouse, Peter speaks with the Lost Boys from the pirate ship. "You need to go back to England. I understand there are families there to adopt all of you. I will return with you and guide the way."

Little Tootles speaks up. "I'll live with Wendy."

Tinker Bell overhears Peter speaking softly, "I kinda wish I had someone."

She senses something strange about the way Peter is acting. "So you'll return right after you get them there…right?"

"Of course! What else would I do, Tinker Bell? Sprinkle the kids, and we'll be off." Peter, the Lost Boys, and Wendy, Michael and John Darling head back through the clouds. With a rainbow flash they disappear from sight.

Tinker Bell follows them for a ways and then turns around for home. After a moment she stops and looks back, again feeling something is wrong. She speaks softly to herself, "Come back quick, Peter."

Chapter 24

Many, Many Years Later

Tinkerbell watches the Rascals from above, but she is thinking about Peter, who has never come back. She lets her mind wander and thinks about Tootles. She then has a bangarang thought and speaks out loud, "I've got it! I'll bring Tootles back! He has always wanted to come back. I know he's getting old, but Neverland can fix that. BANGARANG!"

Off she flies into the clouds. No one notices the rainbow flash she leaves behind.

After a long while, Tinker Bell makes her way to Wendy's house and lands on the balcony. She peeks through the French window and sees that the bedroom door is open. Lights shine from down below. She flies down, looking into the windows, ever-careful not to be seen. Flying from window to window, she finally sees Tootles sitting in his chair. She gently taps on his window, trying to be as quiet as possible. Tootles is dozing off and doesn't hear her.

With little patience left, Tinker Bell finally bangs on the glass. Tootles awakens with a jolt, looks around, and sees the glow from the window. "What is this?" He walks toward the window and sees Tinker Bell. With excitement and glee he opens the window, and Tinker Bell flies in, glowing with excitement to see her old friend. "Tinker Bell, oh, Tinker Bell, I'm so glad to see you! But why are you here?"

She shoots up to his face and pokes his nose. "Want to come back to Neverland?"

"Go back? Is it possible? I am so old now."

She points her finger at him. "Not with my fairy dust, and you know what Neverland can do for you."

Tootles thinks for a moment. "Well… I don't know. Let me think about it…Okay!"

Tinker Bell crosses her arms. "That didn't take much thinkin'. I brought the bag you left behind. Go to the balcony and sprinkle my dust, and off you go. Wait awhile 'til I'm long gone. Tell Wendy so she doesn't worry about you."

"Okay, Tinker Bell, and thank you for coming back for me. Oh, my! I'm going back… I'm really going back!"

*　*　*　*

Tootles waits for about an hour and then calls down to Wendy. "Wendy, Wendy, come up to the bedroom where the balcony is! I have something to tell you."

Wendy is a little surprised, because Tootles has gotten very slow with age, and he is getting a little mentally slow, too. "What in the world do you want me up there for, Tootles?"

Although Wendy is a little older, she is in better shape than Tootles, but she notices that he is much more alert and energetic than usual as he stands in front of the stained-glass window at the top of the stairs. "Just come on up and see."

Wendy is a little irritated. "Don't tell me you found your bag again!"

"Oh, yes. That I did."

Wendy puts her hands up. "Here we go again."

They enter the bedroom. Tootles opens the French window. Wendy feels the cold air rushing in from outside. "Why in the world are you opening the doors? Close them!"

"Come over here and look at the brightest star on the right! That's where I'm going tonight!"

"Those days are over, Tootles. That bag of fairy dust you keep looking for is not here. This has got to stop."

"Yes it is! Tinker Bell brought it here tonight."

Wendy, frustrated, turns to walk away.

"Wendy, wait. It's true! It's BANGARANG!"

Upon hearing that word, she has to turn around, not having heard it in years.

"I'm off to Neverland," Tootles declares. "Thank you for everything you've done, and I hope to see you there."

At that moment Poppy walks into the room. "What's all the fuss about?"

Now Wendy thinks Tootles is really getting worse. "Oh, Tootles—" but before she could finish her sentence he speaks up again.

"I'm off!" He pulls out his bag, sprinkles the fairy dust on himself, steps onto the balcony, and up and away he goes as he catches his foot on the railing and does a somersault in the air. He looks back at Wendy. "No worries."

Wendy is so startled she doesn't know what to do. She walks out onto the balcony, and all she can do now is wave goodbye as Tootles turns, waves back to her, and slowly disappears into the starry sky. Wendy stands there with her hand on her heart and watches him until he is gone.

"Oh, how I've forgotten everything. I'm so happy for you, Tootles. THT!"

Chapter 25

Tootles Returns to Neverland

Some time later in Neverland, off in the near distance from the treehouse, a rainbow light flashes like a sound wave as an object covered in fairy dust breaks through the sparkling multi-colored clouds. Tain spots the flash off in the distance, but it is too far away for him to figure out what is coming down. He walks slowly toward the object. Then he calls out to the others, who follow. Standing together, they see someone somersaulting and hollering.

Shocked and surprised, Tain shouts, "It's a person!"

Puff tilts his head and strains to see. "Who is that?"

They all run toward the person as he crash-lands into the sand on the bluff. As they approach, they see an old man with his face covered in sand. He spits the words out with the sand, "It's me! Tootles!"

But the Rascals don't recognize him, because they have never seen Tootles as an older man. They only briefly remember him from their fight with Hook to rescue the Lost Boys before Peter flew them to England with Wendy, Michael and John Darling, whose parents adopted Tootles and the boys.

Tootles brushes more sand from his face and mumbles as he spits more sand out of his mouth. Once his face is clean, he stands up and stretches out his arms to greet them. "It's me! Tootles!"

The Rascals still can't make him out, but Tootles is excited and happy to be back in Neverland nonetheless. "BANGARANG, all! I'm finally back!"

"How do you know BANGARANG?" Hawkins points at Tootles.

"I be Tootles!" he says with a hearty laugh and his arms outstretched to them again.

They all look at each other in bewilderment for a short, anxious moment. Ambo moves closer to him, leaning forward to look into his face. "You're too old to be Tootles. He was one of the Lost Boys. But yet, there is some resemblance, it seems."

Tootles, realizing so much time has passed, hardly knows what to say. "I grew up with Wendy. Remember, I told Peter I would live with Wendy."

Ambo looks at the others. "Yes, Tootles did say that."

Puff steps forward and points at Tootles. "No way! You can't be Tootles. You're a grownup, and all grownups are pirates!"

Crane jumps forward and taps his sword. "We kill pirates!"

Tootles notices that Puff also has his hand on his sword and becomes a bit nervous. "Pirate? I'm no pirate! I'm Tootles!"

Puff pulls his sword and says softly but sternly, "If you're Tootles, prove it! And you better make it fast!"

Ambo jumps to Tootles' side and places her hand on her sword, stopping the boys in their tracks. "Let's give him time to show us!"

Puff looks at Ambo's determined face. Not wanting to argue with her, he speaks up. "Well, okay, then."

"Jolly good, then! Follow me, and I'll prove I'm Tootles!"

Puff keeps his sword pointed at Tootles as he follows. They all follow along behind Puff. Crane asks Big C, "Could this really be Tootles?"

Puff gives a little laugh and looks at Big C. "Humph! How can this be

Tootles?"

Tain says, "Stranger things have happened here. Ambo has a sense that he is. She is right a lot of the time."

"This would take the cake!" says Big C. "A three-layer."

Tain just chuckles. "We'd better make sure, just in case he is Tootles. Ha! I'd like a three-layer."

They both laugh.

Chapter 26

"If Tinker Bell Says You Are..."

Tootles walks up to the treehouse trunk as Puff puts his sword up against Tootles' chest. "Get to showin' us."

Nervously, Tootles reaches around and points to the secret door-opener. "See, no need to be violent. I be Tootles."

Surprised, Crane points at him. "Hey…he knows the secret!"

Puff, also surprised, steps back, curiously eyeing Tootles up and down. "Is that really you, Tootles? Really?"

Ambo steps in with her arms crossed and her eyebrow up, Tinker Bell-style. "I told you I thought it was Tootles."

Just then, Tinker Bell flies down between Puff and Tootles. "Oh, Tootles! Glad to see you!"

The Rascals just look at each other, dumbfounded, before turning their gazes back toward Tootles and Tinker Bell. Puff shrugs his shoulders. "If Tinker Bell says you are really Tootles, then I guess you are! But how did you get here?"

Tinker Bell folds her arms and shakes her head. "Fairy dust, of course!" With one eyebrow raised she mouths the word "Dummy" and flies away.

"Tinker Bell brought me fairy dust in my old bag. I shook it out, and I was off to the brightest star on the right. BANGARANG, and double BANGARANG!"

Tinker Bell sits on a tree-limb above the Rascals and rests her chin on her hands. "Well, duh! Isn't that what I just said?"

Puff is still a bit confused as he stares at Tootles. "For sure you're Tootles, but what happened to you?"

"Yeah, I know. I'm afraid it's called aging, just like it happened to Peter. Peter is grown up and has a family of his own now."

Puff stares at him with a strange look of disbelief. "Peter is grown up?"

All of the Rascals look at each other in astonishment. Whippy looks especially confused. "I didn't think that was possible."

Tootles turns to Whippy. "One thing about Peter, though, he didn't age like the rest of us. It must be his ties to Neverland. I was getting so old I thought I'd lost my bag of fairy dust and marbles."

"We can get you another bag if you like," Hawkins says.

After a moment of silence, Tootles laughs. "You know…the marbles in my head."

The Rascals laugh at his sense of humor. Puff chuckles, turns to the rest of the group, and introduces Tootles for the first time. "This is Neverland's very own Tootles! Hot chocolate for everyone! This is quite a day to celebrate!"

A few of the boys run off to get more hot chocolate. Just as they return, Brown Cow and Tall Tree appear and approach Tootles. Brown Cow crosses his arms, stands in front of Tootles, gives him a once-over, and raises his right arm in greeting. "Ugh!"

Tootles is confused. " 'Ugh'? I remember 'ugh,' but I still don't know what it means."

Tall Tree leans forward and whispers loudly, "Me don't know either. He always says that. We glad you here. Welcome home."

They all cheer and hug him, welcoming him back to Neverland. Tootles and the Rascals dance and jump around as they head toward the table in great excitement. Puff and Tootles jump up on the table and dance together while the rest of the boys make a circle around the table, dancing and clapping. After a few moments, Puff and Tootles jump down from the table and toast with mugs of hot chocolate.

Tootles is not even out of breath. "Just being here makes me feel young again!"

Puff points at Tootles. "Pretty spry for an old man, too."

Tinker Bell flies down between them and hovers there with that same arrogant look on her face. "It's the fairy dust!"

Puff and Tootles stare at each other for a second and burst out laughing as Tinker Bell flies off in a huff. The celebration continues as they clink their mugs together. Everyone is dancing around, celebrating Tootles' return. Some jump up on the table and down again, others skip in circles, and still others do cartwheels.

Chapter 27

Grown Up in a Rut

Many years have passed, and Peter Pan, the boy who didn't want to grow up, is now a responsible husband, father and hard worker. Yet his aging has been slow, due to his ties to Neverland.

Peter sits at his desk and intently watches his co-workers through the glass walls of his office as they bustle around doing their jobs. Unable to concentrate on his own work, he begins to daydream…

* * * *

The Rascals are sword-fighting with Hook, thrusting back-and-forth several times until Hook mortally wounds one of them. Peter runs to the fallen Rascal and kneels down beside him. With his dying breath the Rascal gasps, "Put an end to Hook."

Peter stands up and stares at Hook with fiery hatred in his eyes. Hook waves his sword in the air, laughs, jumps forward, and thrusts it toward Peter.

* * * *

The phone rings, snapping Peter back to reality. He rubs his face and reaches for the phone. With a sigh he answers it as Mary, a young woman, walks into his office, holding paperwork up in the air. "Peter, all these need to—"

Peter puts his hand up to silence her, points to the phone, and motions for her to wait. Another co-worker, Jack, bursts into the office, pushes his way past the young woman, slams his hands on Peter's desk and leans over it toward him. "What about the Johnson story?"

Now Peter is totally frustrated by the phone conversation and the interruptions. "What is it that can't wait 'til I'm off the phone?"

He glares at Jack, who tries to diffuse the tension. "We need some headlines, dude, and not the kind you get from sleeping on corduroy pillowcases."

Finding no humor in Jack's comment, Peter slowly and deliberately stands up, quickly reaches a hand across the desk, grabs Jack by the ear, and without letting go walks around the desk and pulls him by the ear to the door.

"Hey, hey, that's my ear!" Jack cries out in pain.

Peter agrees. "And here's a headline for you. You're very ear-i-tat-ing!"

Peter shoves Jack through the door and turns around to face Mary, who is so shocked by Peter's actions she is unable to speak. Holding the papers up like a shield, she backs out of the office and bumps into an intern looking for Peter.

"The boss wants to know what you're going to do about the Johnson story," the intern says.

Peter shakes his head. "There's so much going on right now, so much stress, I have no idea!"

The intern sighs. "I know what you mean. Sometimes I wish I could just fly away."

Realizing what the young man just said, Peter looks up with a stunned expression and stares at him without batting an eye.

"Peter, are you okay?"

There is no response as Peter continues to stare, as if in some other world. The intern leaves Peter's office and goes into the boss's office. Peter is now sitting at his desk as if in a trance as his boss enters. He stands there for a few moments and finally breaks the silence: "Peter, are you okay?"

Startled, Peter jumps up. His boss, startled by Peter's sudden movement, takes a self-defense posture. In response, Peter jerks back, lifting his hands to defend himself. An awkward silence follows. Peter sits down and takes a deep breath.

"Peter, I'm really worried about you. You're just not yourself these days."

"I'll be okay, I think," Peter responds mournfully.

"Peter, your odd behavior is affecting everyone in the office. Do you want to talk about it?"

Peter puts his head down on the desk. "It isn't anything I can talk to you about."

His boss frowns and leans closer to Peter. "I think you need some time off—again—to get your head together."

With a sigh, Peter agrees. "Maybe you're right."

"Get yourself together. Fix whatever it is that's wrong, and then come back to work. We need you here, but we need all of you—body and mind, all intact." His boss shakes his head as he leaves the office.

Peter remains at his desk for a bit, then picks up a handful of papers and wads them up in his hand. He stands, shakes his head, and slumps back into his chair. Holding out the papers, he stares blankly at them as a shadow of sadness covers his face.

Sighing deeply, he mutters, "I hate Hook. He kills children."

Chapter 28

A Great Idea

Trish, Peter's wife, is in the kitchen cooking dinner while the children run around the table playing tag. They get a little out of control, as children do. Slowing them down a bit, Trish says, "Your father will be home soon. Why don't you go and clean up for dinner?"

Clint slows down and sniffs the air. "Yeah, it smells good, and I'm hungry."

Amber, his older sister by two years, can't slow down soon enough. Bumping into Clint, she nods her head. "Me, too!"

The children continue playing as they leave the kitchen to wash up for dinner. Peter enters quietly through the back kitchen door behind Trish. The sound of the door closing startles her. Frightened for a moment, she puts her hands on her chest and then realizes Peter is home.

"Peter, you startled me! You shouldn't sneak in the back door like that. Aren't you a little early today?"

Peter laughs. "I'm not sneakin'. I just wanted to surprise you!"

Trish is still a little shaken. "Well, you surprised me all right, but I call it sneaking."

Peter cracks a shy smile. "Sneakin'! I wasn't sneakin'."

Trish knows she has him, and she laughs. "Then what were you doing?"

"I was sneakin'."

They laugh and hug hello. Trish is still curious. "So why are you home this early?"

Peter stands akimbo. "The surprise is that my boss gave me some time off for good behavior."

Trish imitates her husband's posture. "So he sent you home again, did he?"

Peter's guilty grin gives way to the moment of reality as he lowers his head, shrugging his shoulders. He paces up and back with his hands in his pockets. He stops across the table from Trish and smiles. "Trish, I have a great idea!"

Trish turns back to the stove, skeptical. "Oh, sure, let's hear it."

Peter grins from ear to ear. "Let's go back to Grammy Wendy's for a visit. The kids don't have school right now, and maybe a visit will help clear my head."

Pleasantly surprised, Trish spins around and holds out her arms. "What a truly great idea! Grammy Wendy is getting up in years, and besides, the kids love it there."

They hug as they dance around the kitchen table. The children return and see this spectacle. They glance at each other, rolling their eyes. Clint cocks his head to one side. "What's all the excitement about?"

Peter and Trish stop celebrating and wink at each other. Crossing his arms, Peter pretends to be serious. "We have decided to send you both to bed without dinner."

Clint is a little uncertain. "Na-uh."

Peter chuckles. "No. We've decided to go to England again, to see Grammy Wendy. What do you think?"

Clint and Amber jump up and down in excitement. They dance in circles as they high-five each other. Clint imitates his dad by putting his hands on his hips. "Back to Peter Pan Land! Yippee!"

Peter reminds them, "You know, you two aren't to say anything to anyone about that. It's our secret. Besides, they'll just think you're crazy."

Clint giggles. "Okay, Dad, we'll just act normal."

Wary of that impish giggle, Peter turns away, and the children shoot mischievous grins at each other. He spins around, trying to catch them, but they just give him a wide-eyed innocent look. "Acting normal is what concerns me," he says. "Ha!" Then he says under his breath, "Oh, to be a kid again. No stress or guilt to deal with. Why did I have to grow up?"

"What's that about growing up?"

Not realizing Trish has been standing right behind him, Peter jumps at the sound of her voice. Then he softly answers, "Nothing, Trish. Nothing."

"Whatever 'nothing' is, it's affecting your work, and us too, especially when you get moody for no apparent reason."

He doesn't want to acknowledge her statement, so he smiles and gives her a hug. "We have to get organized for Merry Ol' England, you know."

Trish squints her eyes. "It's not working. Don't change the subject."

Peter smiles and hugs her again.

Chapter 29

To Peter Pan Land

The big day has come. The suitcases have been packed and loaded into the trunk of the taxi. Peter is anxious to get started. He calls the children, "Let's get going! We don't want to miss the plane!"

They come running downstairs like a herd of cattle. Everyone climbs into the cab. Peter sits up front with the driver. As they drive off, Clint rolls down his window, points forward, and yells out the window, "To Peter Pan Land!"

Peter quickly turns toward the back seat. "Clint, I said to keep it a secret."

Clint slumps back in the seat and whispers, "To Peter Pan Land."

Amused by his son's whisper, he smiles at Trish and boldly proclaims, "To Peter Pan Land!"

They all laugh, except the taxi driver, who seems a bit confused.

*   *   *   *

The sun is beginning to set. Rays are shining through the windows of Wendy's home, giving it a warm, cozy feeling, even though snow is on the ground. Wendy is sitting on the sofa before the fireplace. Poppy, Wendy's friend, is in the Queen Anne chair. The tea-table is between them with a fresh brewed pot of tea and a dish of homemade crumpets.

Wendy smiles as she sips her tea. "I can hardly wait for Peter and family to get here. I even miss the adventures some, Neverland and all of it. I've never told anyone, but I do, sometimes."

Poppy is surprised. "What about Hook? Do you miss Hook?"

Wendy sits down her teacup. "Heavens, no! I've never met anyone so evil. He said he was Neverland! That's not so." She stops in thought and takes a deep breath. "Neverland is Neverland. No one person or one anything can change it."

Poppy nods her head in agreement. "I think I understand. Everyone in Neverland is part of Neverland."

Wendy changes the subject as she takes another sip of tea and a bite of crumpet. "Do you remember Tootles always looking for his bag? It wasn't so funny then."

"But now that you mention it, it was a little funny thinking back, crawling on the floor looking for it. I hope he's happy back in Neverland. I'm so glad he was able to go. I was never totally convinced of Neverland, but when I saw Tootles leave, well, that did it."

Wendy sets her cup on the table and gets up to stand in front of the fire. "I'm going to lay down for a bit. Would you let me know when they get here, and wake me if I'm sleeping?"

Poppy nods. "You know it will be awhile. They won't be here until later tonight."

Wendy goes upstairs as Poppy tidies the living room.

Chapter 30

Truffle Trouble at Heathrow

Later that night, outside Heathrow Airport, Peter loads his family's luggage into a taxi. Trish and the children are inside the terminal, watching in amazement as the taxi driver, George, sits there eating chocolate-covered truffles, not even attempting to assist Peter.

The luggage is finally loaded, and Peter brushes the snow from his coat. He is momentarily distracted by a group of teens in strange dress. Without thinking about the driver side being opposite in England, he opens the door and plunks down right into George's lap. Two of his truffles land on the passenger seat. Silence ensues, and then George and Peter stare at each other and realize what's happened. Trish and the children laugh hysterically.

In his attempt to jump out of the taxi, Peter whacks his head on the doorframe, which knocks him right back into George's lap. Everyone laughs as Peter rubs his head and lifts himself out. George, however, finds absolutely no humor in the incident and is more than a little irritated as he spews, "Hey, watch it, mate!"

Peter sees the crushed truffles in the driver's lap and again bursts out laughing until he realizes the chocolate mess is undoubtedly on the back of his coat. As he brushes its backside, he feels the melted chocolate and decides to take the coat off. He opens the passenger door, plops down into the seat, and jumps out of the taxi in the same movement. The truffles that flew from George's hand are now a squashed chocolate mess all over Peter's rear end and the passenger seat.

Trish and the children burst into laughter again, and this time the driver laughs, too. "You sure makin' a mess, mate."

Peter, although embarrassed, tries to make light of it. "Yuck, chocolate… I don't even like chocolate."

Clint, still laughing, sings, "Dad has a chocolate butt!"

Amber, bending over in laughter, slaps Clint on the knee and repeats, "Chocolate butt! Chocolate butt!"

Trish notices a change in Peter's look and warns the children, "Settle down. I don't think your father appreciates your teasing."

Peter, obviously irritated, pulls the squashed truffles from his pants. A melted chocolate mess is now stuck to his hand, and there is no place to throw it away. Leaning in and looking at the driver, Peter extends his hand to get some help. George hesitates, then pulls out a paper napkin and carefully removes the mess from Peter's hand. With a saddened face George stares at the squashed truffles in the napkin and up at Peter. "Me poor misses, she slaved over them truffles."

Peter is still embarrassed. "Sorry, mate." He re-enters the taxi, sheepishly looks at George, and closes the door. The taxi pulls away from the stand, and they're finally off to Wendy's house.

The snow is no longer falling when the taxi pulls up in front of Grammy Wendy's. George helps Trish and the children out. After helping Peter with the luggage, he notices the chocolate on the passenger door.

Peter hands him a five-dollar tip. George throws his hands in the air. "You sure you can afford that, mate?" He shakes his head, gets in and pulls away, leaving the family and luggage on the curb.

The family watches as the taxi disappears down the road. Peter waves and laughs, "That driver wouldn't even take a fiver!"

Trish chuckles and shrugs her shoulders. "Can't really blame him. You made that awful chocolate mess, and to add insult to injury you only offer him the five-dollar tip."

Peter finally gets it and starts to laugh. Clint changes his song: "Dad's a cheap chocolate butt!"

Trish shakes her head and motions for them to come up the walkway.

GRAMMY WENDY

Chapter 31

At Grammy's House

As the family walks up to Grammy Wendy's front door, Peter sternly says to Clint, "Stop chewing your gum. And remember, this is Good Manners Land."

Clint, with a little attitude, responds, "Okay, Dad, I'll remember."

Peter quickly glances back to see if he can catch Clint's usual mischievous look. "And no funny stuff." He ruffles Clint's hair and turns to knock on Wendy's door.

As soon as Peter's back is turned, Clint, with a wicked chuckle, puts his gum in Amber's hair. Recognizing that laugh, she spins around and glares at Clint with squinty, suspicious eyes. "Whatever it is, don't even think about it!" Clint just smiles.

Peter is poised to knock on the door again as the door flies open. Poppy appears in the doorway and greets them with a happy little, "Aahhh, you finally made it!" as she hugs them all. She is so excited at their arrival she forgets to close the door, so Peter walks back to do the honors. As he stands in the doorway, he looks up at the stars, focuses on the brightest one for a brief minute, and slowly closes the door.

As he passes the staircase on his way back to the living room, he sees Wendy at the top of the stairs in front of the large stained-glass window.

"How was the flight, Peter?"

He climbs up to give her a hug. "I think I'm getting used to flying." They chuckle as Peter holds her by the arm and guides her down the steps.

Trish meets them on the stairs and greets Wendy with a big hug. Taking her arm from Peter, she guides Wendy down. Peter, still standing where Trish met them on the steps, turns back and stares motionlessly through the window. His memory takes him beyond the full moon, and he sees himself flying in the night sky with Tinker Bell. The reminiscences flood his mind. He is so taken back by his thoughts of Hook he literally has to grab the railing to guide himself back down the stairs. At the bottom, anger rolls over him as he clenches his fists and mutters, "I hate Hook."

*   *   *   *

Everyone gathers in the kitchen. It is a typical English kitchen, with everything in its proper place. Amber is standing in front of the sink while Trish and Poppy try to get the gum out of her hair. "Ouch! Please don't pull so hard."

Trish finally decides it is best to cut the gum out. "Sorry, Amber, but we're going to have to cut your hair some."

Amber turns and glares at Clint. "It's all your fault. I wanted my hair to be long and pretty." She tears up as Clint giggles.

"This isn't funny, Clint." Trish is frustrated herself. "Clint, you know better than to play these foolish pranks. This time it's quite serious, young man."

"You ought to be punished for putting the gum in my hair!" Amber cries.

Peter, who has been quietly observing Clint's attitude, finally steps in with a tone of authority. "You're supposed to be on your best behavior, Clint. Did you already forget what I told you?"

Clint hangs his head, embarrassed. "No, sir. This is England, the land of good manners."

"Silly pranks are part of growing up," Wendy says, "but gum in your sister's hair?"

Clint feels more remorse. "I'm sorry, Grammy Wendy. I guess I should grow up a little."

Wendy puts her arm around him. "Well, don't grow up while you're here. As a matter of fact, that goes for all of you—that's the law." She points toward the living room. "Cocoa's ready! Everyone get your mug, and let's take it out to the living room. We can all relax and enjoy it in there. And you, Sir Clint, be a dear and put some extra wood on the fire."

Clint, hoping this would help his image, replies with due respect, "Yes, ma'am."

Chapter 32

Shadowy Pirates

Everyone is sitting in the cozy room, enjoying hot cocoa. Grammy Wendy guides Amber to the footstool in front of the fireplace, which now fills the room with warmth. The brightness of the fire casts flickering shadows as the family moves around in front of it, warming themselves up. Peter fixates on the shadowy silhouettes on the wall. Once again, his memories of Hook well up in his head. In his mind, the shadows take on the form of pirates, sword-fighting, and the horror of Hook's cruelty to the Lost Boys. Peter is in his own world, dark and lonely, as if in a deep trance.

Grammy brushes Amber's hair. "You know Amber, your hair is still very beautiful."

Amber turns and glares at Clint, who shrugs his shoulders and shouts, "What?"

Startled by Clint's voice, Peter realizes his thoughts have drifted far away. Pretending to have been listening, he raises his mug and interjects an official opinion: "Mmmm, this is really good Po Po."

Trish curiously looks over at Peter and smiles as she notices the cocoa on his upper lip. "Po Po? What's Po Po?"

"I mean cocoa." Peter approaches the mirror on the wall and checks out his Po Po mustache. Smirking at his reflection in the mirror, he wipes his upper lip. "It's late, and we all need to get to bed."

Trish and Wendy gently guide the children to the steps, in spite of their groaning and objections. Halfway up the steps, Clint stops and stares at the moonlit window. Amber comes up right behind him, takes his hand and whispers, "It's okay, Clint. They were just scary stories. Hook is gone."

Trish is close enough to hear the word 'gone.' "What's gone?"

Clint and Amber ignore her question and run up the stairs together. Trish is still wondering what they were talking about. "Amber? Clint?"

From the top of the stairs they reply, "Nothing, Mom."

Clint and Amber's bedroom is quite unique. Its walls are replete with colorful murals depicting Neverland, Captain Hook, Peter Pan, pirates, and some of the Lost Boys. A heavy French door opens out to the balcony. Twin light sconces softly glow over each bed. An antique China doll rests on the nightstand by Amber's bed.

Trish and Wendy turn down the blankets and fluff the pillows, preparing the beds for the children. Amber is already in her pajamas, sitting on her bed. Clint enters the room in his pajamas but stops and stares at the mural depicting Captain Hook.

Trish motions toward Clint's bed. "Come on, Clint, hop into bed."

The life-sized Hook in the mural makes him nervous as he passes the balcony door. "Is the door locked?"

"Yes, it is. But there's no need to worry. Remember, Hook is gone."

Clint slowly climbs into bed. "I know, Mom, but some of the stories are scary. Especially the ones where he kidnaps children still have me just a little scared."

Wendy and Trish settle the children into bed. "Hook is dead," Trish tells them, "and Peter is here to protect you anyway."

Clint looks up at his mother. "Oh, yeah, Peter Pan, my dad."

Chapter 33

The Antique Little Girl

Wendy is sitting on the edge of Amber's bed. She reaches over for the antique China doll on the nightstand, holds it close to her heart, and hands it to Amber, who smiles and takes the doll. "Grammy Wendy, are you too old to play with dolls?"

Wendy sighs. "I've grown up on the outside, but inside I'm still like a little girl."

Amber returns the doll to her Grammy, who smiles and sets it in her own lap. "I guess you could say that I'm an antique little girl." She begins to sing:

> *Antique Little Girl*
>
> *I am the same little girl I was long ago.*
>
> *Time is like a rising mist—where does it go?*
>
> *It flies like lightning as years twist and whirl.*
>
> *Within me, you will find an antique little girl.*
>
> *When I was your age, I would run and play*
>
> *Hopscotch and dolls, in fond yesterdays.*
>
> *Older on the outside, to the whole world,*
>
> *But within me you will find an antique little girl.*
>
> *Oh somewhere deep inside, I'm an antique little girl.*

I'd love to play with you all day,

But so many things always get in the way.

Somewhere deep inside, youth hides like a pearl.

I am certain you will find an antique little girl.

Unlike this china doll, that won't change.

My heart remains in Neverland, my body's rearranged,

My soul craves adventure, in that magic world.

Somewhere deep inside I'm an antique little girl.

Wendy gently caresses the doll and smiles at Amber, then leans over and kisses her on the forehead. Amber smiles and closes her eyes. "I love you, Grammy Wendy."

Wendy places the antique doll back on the nightstand and gently tucks Amber in. "I love you very much."

Trish tucks in Clint and kisses him on the cheek. "I love you very much."

Clint, being a boy, replies, "Yeah, me too, Mom."

As Wendy and Trish turn to leave the room, they see Clint wiping his cheek, as if he were given a sloppy, wet kiss. They glance at each other, chuckle and say goodnight.

Chapter 34

Words of Wisdom

Peter fixes himself another mug of Po Po and says to himself "Just one, just one more mug."

Wendy and Trish enter the living room and see the mug in Peter's hand. Grammy smiles as Trish jokes, "He's just a Co Co-a-holic."

Smiling at the humor, Peter lifts his mug. "Cheers." He turns toward Trish. "I'm going upstairs to check on the kids," He marches past them.

Wendy looks at Trish. "Peter sure keeps a watch out for the kids, doesn't he?"

"Yes, Peter has decided to spend more time with the kids before they get older."

"There is nothing more important than the time you spend with each other. You can sometimes get money or other things back, but you can never get back the time you wasted."

"Words of wisdom, Grammy Wendy, but there still seems to be something wrong with Peter. His boss made him take this time off to get himself straightened out."

"We'll talk with Peter tomorrow. I think I may know what's wrong."

"Thanks, Grammy Wendy, but he just won't talk about it. Every time I try, he makes a joke of it and changes the subject."

*   *   *   *

Upstairs, Peter enters the children's room to find Clint and Amber asleep. Moonlight beams through the window, contrasting with the soft yellow glow of the lamps, causing the murals to take on a surrealistic lifelike appearance. The moonlight casts Peter's shadow on the mural. He tightly grips the mug in his hand and stares intently at the wall, where the characters appear to be moving.

Motionless, Peter is lost in a flashback. The sounds of seagulls and pirates dueling begin to fill the room. He thinks back to when he was restrained by two pirates as Hook ordered two of the Lost Boys to walk the plank blindfolded with their hands tied from behind.

Suddenly, Peter snaps out of it. He takes a big gulp from the mug, sets it on the dresser, tiptoes toward the beds and checks out the children, as if guarding them from danger. Finding them sleeping peacefully, he turns to face the Hook character on the mural, points to it, and whispers, "Never, ever again will you harm any more children."

Peter is apprehensive as he approaches the French window. After eyeing the handle for a moment, he opens the window, steps out onto the balcony, places his arms akimbo, and declares, "I hate the very memory of Hook."

He steps backward into the room, closes and locks the window, and sees the rocking chair rock itself. He walks toward it and decides the breeze from closing the door rocked it, but remembers that the door was already closed. Confused, he looks up at the mural of Hook, glances back at the door, shrugs his shoulders, settles himself into the rocker, closes his eyes and begins to drift off. "Neverland, Tinker Bell…"

Not quite asleep, Peter jolts back to reality. Resting his head against the back of the rocker, he stares at the ceiling. "I do miss Neverland and Tinker Bell. We sure had some great adventures, didn't we, Tinker?" His eyes close and he falls asleep, not waking up when that same strange breeze from nowhere, like magic, lightly ruffles his hair.

Some time later, Trish finds Peter asleep in the rocker. She checks on the kids and then wakes him. Half asleep, he walks down the stairs to bed. Tricia follows him, quietly closing the door behind her so as not to wake the children. Peter is so exhausted from travel and stress he crawls into bed.

Just before sunrise, Peter gets up and walks back upstairs to check on the kids. All is well, and he returns to the rocker and falls asleep in it again.

Chapter 35

An English Breakfast

The morning sun rises and streams through the window, slowly moves down Peter's forehead, and finally shines in his eyes, waking him. Stiff from sleeping in the rocker, he groans, "Ahhhh!" As he gets up he stretches his back, shakes himself fully awake, and straightens his clothes. He checks the still-sleeping children before leaving the room.

Peter smiles broadly as the aroma of good cooking wafts through the doorway. He goes downstairs and enters the kitchen to see Grammy Wendy preparing breakfast and Trish seated at the table. "Good morning, and a good morning it is," he says happily.

"Good morning, Peter," the women respond in unison.

Trish kisses Peter on the cheek, "Are the children okay?" She knows all is well but wants to make Peter feel better.

"BANGARANG! I mean, yes, yes, they're fine."

Clint and Amber are awakened by the delicious aroma of breakfast and head down the stairs, still in their pajamas. After hugs all around, they excitedly chatter about Neverland. "We are really here in Peter Pan land," says Clint, his arms akimbo.

Amber is a little less excited. "Yes, we've heard the great adventure stories. Even scary ones, too."

Clint frowns. "Hook was really mean."

"Yeah, very mean," mimics Amber.

Clint struts toward Peter and takes an introductory pose, "My dad—Peter Pan."

Amber hurries over to give Peter a big hug. "Our hero!"

Peter starts to hug Clint, who just lays his head on his father and then heads for the table. "I'm hungry."

Peter chuckles. "That wasn't a hug. I call that a lean."

Tricia gives a little chuckle herself.

Wendy gestures to everyone. "Well, come on then, let's all get to the table."

Peter surveys it and smiles. "Trish, you can see the difference in the kids already. This place seems to bring out the best in us."

"Yes, and it's wonderful. But what about you, Peter?"

Wendy, sensing this is not the time to get into Peter's issues, interrupts. "We can have that discussion later. Right now we need to say grace."

She nods toward Peter, who declares with an impish grin, "Grace!"

Wendy tries not to laugh for the children's sake. "All right Peter, enough of that."

"Yes, ma'am." After a short pause to compose himself, he begins. "Heavenly Father, thank you for the food we are about to receive. Bless the hands that prepared and served it. Bless all at this table. In Jesus' name, Amen."

Chapter 36

Missing Peter in Neverland

At that very moment in Neverland, Tinker Bell thinks out loud as she flies down from the treehouse to the table below, where the Rascals are eating breakfast. "I sure wish Peter were here. Things just aren't the same." She lands on a mug turned upside-down. "We have a lot of fun here with games and great adventures, don't we?"

Puff agrees. "Yeah, lots of fun. Will we ever see Peter again? He has been away for a long, long time. He promised he would be back."

Tinker Bell is a bit irritated. "Peter will never forget us." Her eyes well up with tears as she flies back up to the treehouse so the children can't see her cry. Once inside her cuckoo-clock house, in front of her tiny mirror, she softly sobs. Her teary-eyed reflection in the mirror upsets her even more. "What are you looking at?" Tears run down her little cheeks. "Oh, Peter, where are you? Why don't you come back? We need you. I need you."

Puff, not fooled by her quick departure, looks up at the treehouse and shakes his head. "I think Tinker Bell misses Peter more than she lets on."

Aky is worried too. "Will Tinker Bell be okay?"

Tain tries to act confident. "Sure, she will. Tomorrow we'll play hide and seek. She loves that game."

*   *   *   *

The next morning, when breakfast is ready, mischief is in the air. Hawkins looks around for an unsuspecting target. Finding it, she slowly picks up some cold, clammy oatmeal and hurls it at her victim. SPLAT! And the food-fight is on—food flying everywhere!

Puff, not yet covered in food, tries to put a halt to the rumpus. "Stop! Enough is enough! I want to eat!"

Everyone stops all at once, as if on a time-out. They all sit down, looking at each other and back at Puff. Pinner, grinning from ear to ear, says with a grand gesture, "The Puff has spoken!"

Seconds later, with much nodding and winking at each other, an all-out food assault on Puff begins. Before long he is totally covered from head to toe. Like a mummy, only his eyes can be seen. All the other Rascals are rolling and laughing uncontrollably.

Tinker Bell, hearing all the commotion, steps out of her little house to see what is happening. She sees Puff, immediately begins to laugh hysterically, and accidentally rolls right off the limb and onto a large leaf. Her laughter permeates the air, and the sight of her shenanigans makes the Rascals break into even more riotous laughter.

Soon the kids are laughing so hard tears stream from their eyes. The food covering them mixes with dirt and twigs as they roll around on the ground and hold their sides in hysteria. Aky, realizing just how messy it all was, yells, "Smear fight!"

They jump on each other and rub the mess into each other's hair, face and clothes. The friendly food-fight soon turns into an uncontrollable chain reaction of laughter and frivolity. Tinker Bell, finally getting control of herself, laughs lightly as she watches. "It's still Neverland, even without Peter. Just not as good."

Chapter 37

Hook's Plan

After many years, Hook returns in the night, as he said he would. Smee does not know where Hook went, and no one knows he is back from the dead. Hook and Smee, after a short hello, are sitting in a meeting in Hook's cabin, where he is mapping out his plan.

"I have waited all these years to perfect my plan to get even with that Pan, and now the time is right. Here is a list of supplies we'll need." Hook glares at Smee with a squinty evil eye. "Get someone to collect these supplies so we can start catching those pathetic Rascals."

Smee jumps up from his chair. "Aye-aye, Cap'n, right away! I'll find one of the men to get right on it." He starts to leave, and then turns around and salutes Hook several times. "Hook is back!" Then he leaves the cabin.

Now alone, Hook stands in front of the full-length mirror. Turning this way and that, he primps and admires himself. "I will get Peter Pan! He will pay!"

Smee rounds up Jenks to help get the supplies Hook has ordered. However, he neglects to tell Jenks what or for whom the job is. Jenks follows Smee through the cabin door and does a double take at the sight of Hook. He is so stunned he is frozen in time, blubbering to himself, trying to understand that after all this time Hook is alive, not dead. Fearfully, he starts to back out the door while pointing a shaky hand at Hook.

"Hoooook? Are ye a gggghost? Are me eyes lyin'?"

Smee grabs him and pulls him back into the room. "No, Jenks. It is Hook!"

Jenks is still scared. "How did… How could… It can't be."

Smee understands Jenks' disbelief. "Never mind, lad. Come here to the table and sit down a minute while we finish the list."

Still very uneasy at the sight of Hook, Jenks is about to seat himself in Hook's chair. Hook sees Jenks and rushes over, hooks his shirt by the collar, and pulls him up before his bottom can hit the seat. Then Hook pulls out his knife, lays it against Jenks neck, and casts a threatening evil eye at him. "Arrrrgh! No one sits in Hook's chair!"

Jenks trips backwards and falls on the floor, shoving Hook's chair out of place. Terrified, he gets up and carefully puts the chair back. "Sorry, Cap'n. Really, sorry I am."

Hook and Smee just glare at him. Jenks sees a chair across the cabin and starts toward it. An awkward-looking chair with a slanted, leather-covered hardwood seat, it was obviously made more for looks than comfort, and its lack of padding gives it a slick appearance. Jenks tries to sit in it but slides off, hitting the floor with a thud. Hook and Smee say nothing. Jenks, growling under his breath, gets up and tries it again. The same thing happens, and this time he shows his big ugly teeth in a snarl and his bushy unibrow frown.

By now Hook and Smee are watching him in disgusted disbelief. Smee grabs Jenks, pulls him away before he can start a third time, and points to a large, fluffy chair across the cabin. "Sit in that one, ya fool. Sit and shut."

Jenks makes his way to the chair, lowers himself into it, and sinks down until his face is level with his knees. Arms and legs thrash all about as he tries to lift himself out. He looks around and groans until finally he can get out of the chair. He turns and eyes it with one side of his unibrow up, feels the seat with his hand, and finds it hard as a rock. He stares at the seat for a minute in disbelief. Leaning forward again, he presses both hands, palms down, on the seat, only to find it still as hard as a rock. He stares at it again, scratching his head as he tries to figure out how he could have sunk so far into it. Just for good measure, Jenks makes a fist and pounds the seat, only to experience its hardness again. Shaking his hand in pain, he decides it's hard enough to sit on, and as he does he promptly sinks down again. Only his unibrow and eyes can be seen, just over his knees.

Hook and Smee gaze at each other in incredulity again. Hook is now impatient with Jenks' antics. "Jenks! Enough! I'm warnin' ya!"

Shook up, Jenks tries to get out of the chair, but his arms and legs again go flying. Finally he gets himself up, but, alas, as he backs away from the chair, he steps on his own foot, trips, and falls on Smee, who grabs him and puts him in front of Hook's desk.

Hook, too frustrated to speak, simply groans as he hands Smee the final list. He then taps his sword and glares at Jenks as Smee passes the list onto him. "You are to tell no one, Jenks, do you understand? Tell no one about me. No one is to know Hook is back."

Jenks understands the meaning of Hook's sword and nods fearfully. Smee, a bit less intimidating, points to some of the items on the list. "We need these items right away."

Jenks scans the list with a big, nervous smile. "Okay, then." He turns it upside down and sideways and then flips it over.

Hook cocks his head to one side and watches Jenks. "What exactly are you doing?"

Embarrassed, Jenks grins shyly, "Well, ya see, Cap'n… I never… I don't… I mean, Cap'n, sir, I… I can't read."

Hook is furious. "Smee!"

Smee grabs Jenks by the collar and drags him outside and out of Hook's sight.

*   *   *   *

Later that afternoon, Jenks and Sparky are peeling potatoes. Jenks looks around and leans over to whisper into Sparky's ear. "This is top secret, but I know I can trust you. Hook's got plans to capture Peter Pan."

Sparky looks up at Jenks with his eyebrows raised. "Huh? What are ye saying?"

Jenks checks all around to make sure no one can hear him and whispers, "Yeah Sparky, Hook really isn't dead, and he got a plan."

Sparky rolls his eyes, shakes his head and groans. "Never work. We're doomed."

Jenks is a little frustrated with Sparky's attitude. "Why are ye always so negative?"

Sparky just looks at him, goes back to peeling potatoes, and repeats in a low monotone, "Dooomed."

Jenks throws down his potato and gives Sparky a dirty look.

Sparky keeps his head and eyes down and continues to peel, letting out a low "Lurch" type of groan: "Uuuggghhh."

Jenks takes his potato back and continues to peel with a little grunt in order to get in the last word.

Chapter 38

The Pampered Hook

Hook's cabin has luxurious trappings—everything you could think of, and more than anyone could or would ever want. More food than any one or twenty people could possibly consume or would ever eat. Gold, silver and jewels—more treasure than any one or one hundred men could spend in a lifetime.

Hook is sitting in his chair as Smee fluffs a pillow around him. "Smee, I want my smoke. Where is my smoke?"

Smee immediately gets a cigar and holder, taking great care to insert the cigar into the holder so as not to damage the fine tobacco Hook loves so much. Standing in front of Hook, he lights the cigar, takes a puff to be sure it is fresh, and hands it to Hook, who enjoys the cigar's aroma as he sits back in his chair. He takes a puff. In deep thought, he rolls the cigar-holder between his fingers.

"Smee, I have a good plan, and with it, I will capture Peter Pan."

Smee nods. "Cap'n, it's a very good plan. It will work."

Hook raises his hook in the air and gives an evil laugh. "I know. Peter will find out, and when he does, he'll come back. Back to his doom... He is doomed."

Smee looks somewhat confused. "Where have I heard that before?"

"Smee, it's time for my nightcap. Where's my nightcap?"

Smee hurries over to the bedpost, grabs Hook's nightcap, and attempts to remove Hook's wig. "Here y'are, Cap'n, I'll help ya."

Hook grabs Smee's hand to stop him. "No, no. Not that, you idiot. I need my bubbly. Where's my bubbly?"

Smee hurries to the liquor cabinet and takes out a bottle marked Hook's Private Reserve. He uncorks it, takes a big swig, belches, looks cross-eyed, and then smiles broadly as he pours some into a glass for Hook. "Here y'are, Cap'n. Drink up now. It's your bedtime." He helps Hook with his nightgown and cap and tucks him into bed.

Hook acts like a little kid rather than a pirate captain. "Sing me to sleep, Smee."

ROCK-A-BYE CAPTAIN

Rock-a-Bye, Captain, in your bed,
Dreaming of fights, all that are dead.
You always win, it's you they dread.
Rock-a-Bye, Captain, in your bed.
Dreams of past battles abound in your mind.
You're never the loser, you come out fine.
The tip of your saber is quickly fed.
Rock-a-Bye, Captain, in your bed.
Rock-a-Bye, Captain, close your eyes,
Be ready for conflict after sunrise.
Hum you a sea song

To comfort your head.

Rock-a-Bye, Captain, in your bed.

Smee slowly tapers off to a gentle hum and makes sure Hook is asleep. He keeps an eye on Hook as he makes his way back over to the bottle and takes another swig.

Chapter 39

Hook Revealed

Early in the morning, Smee is on deck, watching the motley pirate crew on the dock with their tools waiting for orders. Sparky and Jenks are gathering them together. A large, burly pirate named Jason seems confused about the job at hand. "What's going on? What are we doing? Where are we going?"

Sparky shakes his head. "Uuuuuuh! We're doomed."

Jenks glances up, then back at Sparky. "Negative, negative. Don't be negative!"

The pirates hear this and get a little nervous, which Jenks realizes. "We can count on Hook to see us through."

Now Jason is really confused. "Hook? Hook's been dead a long time now! So how can he help us?"

Another pirate in the crew, Darby by name, says, "Of course, he'd see us through if he were alive, you barnacle-brain! But Hook is dead!"

Jenks realizes he opened his big mouth and turns away, ignoring the pirates.

Smee walks out on the deck, looks below at the Pirates, raises his hands and makes the announcement: "Listen up, ya slimy, slithery sea-snakes! Yer about to be amazed or dazed! Either way, believe what yer eyes tell ya! Rub 'em if ya hafta. Behold, straight from the belly of the croc, the one and only Hooook!"

The pirate crew, as if on cue, all gasp as Hook comes out on deck. Terrified at the sight of him, they talk among themselves, pointing up at Hook. They back off, some in fear, others thinking he's a ghost. Darby rubs his eyes and can't believe what he sees. Then, with a shaky voice, he says, "It's Hook! But it can't be. What trickery is this?"

Oddly, Jason no longer seems confused. "But it is. Hook is back? Truly it is! Hook is back!"

Silence befalls the whole motley crew for several moments as each tries to digest the fact that before them stands the one and only Hook. The silence is broken as one starts to chant, "Hook, Hook, Hook is back!" Then the whole crew joins in. This delights Hook as his ego laps up the praise. After waiting several minutes, Hook lifts his hand to stop the chanting, but when he raises his hook, the pirates start to cheer, "Hook, Hook, alive, alive!"

Hook raises his hand again to quiet the crew, "No one, not anyone, not even the great croc can stop the Hook, because I am Neverland! The Hook will always be Neverland!"

Jason can hardly contain himself as he blurts out loud and clear, "Truly, the Hook is back!"

The chanting and cheering erupt again, but Hook has had enough of the celebration and is ready to get down to the job at hand. He leans forward. "Enough, now! We have a very tough and important mission, but not impossible for me. You'll feel really special about this one."

The pirate Darby is all ears. "A mission? A special mission?"

Hook smugly twists the ends of his mustache. "Yes, our mission is to get

Peter Pan. I will have my revenge, and the Pan is doomed."

The crew once again erupts into cheering and chanting, with even more enthusiasm and excitement. "Hook, Hook, Hook is back! Hook, Hook, Hook is back!" The rhythmic sound delights Hook as he keeps time, twisting his hook to the beat.

Smee tries to quiet them down while encouraging Hook. "D'ya hear it, Cap'n? The men still revere you."

Hook replies with an evil grin, "Yes, and so they should. They are very wise." He leans over to Smee. "Oh, how I do despise these slimy, grimy guppies! Ha!"

Chapter 40

The Pirate Pack Parade

Smee and Jenks, having gathered the items on Hook's list of tools and equipment, order the crew to pack up all they can carry for the journey. They carry heavy nets, buckets, ropes, shovels, picks, water, weapons and the like. All are loaded to the max—all, that is, but Jenks, who has one lonely shovel across his shoulder.

Hook, hand on hip, glares at Jenks. Imitating Hook for effect, Smee also places his hand on his hip and tries to glare, but his chubby face betrays him and makes Jenks laugh heartily. Annoyed, Hook intensifies his glare. The laugh becomes nervous as Jenks realizes Hook's anger.

Pointing to a net left lying on the dock, Hook orders Smee, "Take that net and give it to Jenks!" Smee obediently goes over to the net and picks it up with great difficulty. He can barely carry it to Jenks. As Smee throws the net over Jenks' shoulder, it almost buries him—the weight of the net knocks him to his knees. He groans in pain and struggles to stand up under the weight.

Hook, with great satisfaction and approval, curls up a sadistic smile. "Hmmm, yes." He marches to the head of the pack of pirates and leads them through town. As they tramp through the streets, proudly parading their tools, equipment and netting, they sing:

HOOK IS BACK

Hook is back, Hook is back,

Some be swimmin' in a sack.

Hook is back, Hook is back,

Some will walk the plank.

Hook is back, Hook is back,

You're sad or glad for Neverland

Hook is back, Hook is back,

They've Captain Hook to thank.

A man of evil deeds, stick yee fer the fun of it,

His words pirates heed, Pan would have none of it.

A doer of rotten deeds to be exact.

Look out, look out, Captain Hook is back.

A contemptuous man, no pirate could be bolder,

The villain of Neverland, no sea dog could be colder.

Black heart, evil eyes, he'll give someone a hack

Smee's friend's a bad one, look out, Hook is back

Hook is back, Hook is back,

Some be swimmin' in a sack.

Hook is back, Hook is back,

Some will walk the plank.

Hook is back, Hook is back,

Sad or glad for Neverland

Hook is back, Hook is back,

They've Captain Hook to thank.

Smee said, "Hook, you're back!" while dancing to a
ditty.
In disbelief he stares—his smile wasn't pretty.
Hook watched and twisted while Smee sang this song,
Hook is back, Hook is back, loud and strong.

Townspeople stop what they're doing to see what the singing and chanting is all about. They can't believe their eyes and point in disbelief. More and more come to see. They all join in the chanting and start to follow the pirate pack.

Hook smirks arrogantly and looks back at Smee. "Yes, they are very wise."

His hook is twisting to the tempo of the song as the pirates head off into the wild jungle. Jenks drags the net, brings up the rear, and follows behind Sparky. Some of the townspeople have caught up to the parade and are close behind them. One has accidentally stepped on the trailing net, yanking Jenks down to the ground. Jenks grunts as he struggles to get up. Dismayed, he looks back and gives his unibrow frown.

They march through the trees and thick vines on the path leading deeper into the jungle. High above their heads, Bangarangatang, the Rascals' monkey, annoyed by the chanting, begins to jump and chatter. The sight of Hook's hook reflecting the early morning sun catches the monkey's attention. Screeching, he climbs higher to safety until Hook is out of sight.

As the pirate parade passes under him, Bangarangatang stealthily climbs back down, watching closely as the pirates continue marching. When Sparky passes under him, the monkey almost goes into hysterics—one would swear he is laughing and pointing at the pirate. Sparky looks up and gives a low grunt. The monkey's eyes open wide, and his mouth drops open as Jenks passes under him. Bangarangatang lets out a wild scream and climbs out of sight. Sparky looks around and gives another grunt at Jenks. Frowning, Jenks tries to ignore the monkey. "Just a stupid monkey."

Chapter 41

Cuckoo in the Cuckoo Clock

Meanwhile, inside her cuckoo-clock house, Tinker Bell has just awoke and got out of bed, sitting at her vanity. Although the clock is small, there's plenty of room for her. Staring into the mirror, she thinks out loud, "Where is Peter? Why has he gone for so long? Definitely he's the betterest side of Neverland! Hmmm…and Hook was definitely the worstest, and we're all so glad he's gone. I wish Peter could be here now! We had such great adventures together. Why can't Peter be here now?" In the mirror, she sees a tear falling from her eye. She covers her face with her hands and quietly sobs.

Outside of the clock house, Tootles, Puff, and some of the Rascals are at Tinker Bell's door. Tootles knocks on it and then looks around at the others with a big smile. "Remember! We have to get Tinker Bell to play Hide and Seek with us today."

Puff puts his ear to the door. "Tinker Bell, are you in there?"

From inside, a not too cheerful Tinker Bell answers, "No, I am not here."

Puff looks at Tootles. "Huh?" He turns back to the door. "We're going to play. Why don't you come out and join us?"

"No, not today. I have things to do."

Tootles, like a big kid, puts both hands over his mouth to quiet his laugh. He is confident that, when she hears the game, her very favorite, she will come flying out. "We're going to play Hide and Seek!"

The boys back away from the door, anticipating its bursting open. They giggle as they wait, but nothing happens. Puff cautiously approaches the door. He hears a deep sigh, followed by, "Hide and Seek? No, not today. Maybe tomorrow."

Puff turns to the others. "Gee, Tinker Bell never turns down a game of Hide and Seek."

Tain steps closer to the door. "Are you okay in there, Tinker Bell?"

Now she is getting annoyed. "Yes. I just want to be alone for now."

Tain shrugs his shoulders. "Okay, Tinker, whenever you're ready."

Back at the table under the tree, Puff is the first to break the silence. "I think that Tinker Bell must really miss Peter."

Tain agrees. "I wish he would come back, too."

Whippy shakes his head. "Yeah, we all do. It's funny, but we were never with Peter that long, but it seems like he has always been with us as family."

Chapter 42

The Pit

Meanwhile, at their destination in the jungle under a huge tree, Hook has Jenks and a few others digging a big pit. As they dig, Bangarangatang reappears on a branch high above their heads. He pulls twigs and nuts off the tree and hurls the pieces at Sparky. The monkey's funny-face-laugh is ignited as the twigs and nuts hit their target. He seems delighted with himself as he does back-flips on the branch. Sparky just looks up and grunts. Bangarangatang tosses once again and makes another perfect hit.

Sparky brushes his face and looks up. "Monkey paaaay."

Jenks just laughs.

Shaking a menacing finger at Bangarangatang, Sparky taunts him, "Monkey pay, monkey pay."

"What does that mean?" Jenks asks. "Monkeys don't have gold or silver."

Sparky responds, "It means, monkey pay!"

Jenks shakes his head and continues to work.

Many hours later, the pit is finished. The order to clear and cover it has been given, and everyone climbs out—everyone, that is, except Jenks. He didn't hear the order and is still digging, unaware that the pit is about to be covered. Hook orders the men to cover the pit and disguise it. As they finish dragging the cover over the pit, a voice is heard from underneath. Everyone looks around, wondering who is yelling.

"Hey!" Jenks yells a little louder in the dark.

One pirate gets a little spooked. "Did you hear someone say, 'Hey'? Are there spooks about?"

Jenks, panicking even more, yells even louder, "Hey!"

Hook is walking around the edge of the pit. "Who is that yelling?"

"Hey, I'm down here! Get me out!"

Hook motions for Sparky to pull back the cover and put a ladder down. Waiting impatiently, Hook taps his sword on the ladder. Up comes Jenks, wearing dirt from head to toe. Hook pointes his sword at Jenks throat. "Sooner or later."

Terrified of Hook's sword, Jenks tries to dodge its tip, which causes the ladder to slip just enough to fall back into the pit. Jenks, not letting go, slams to the bottom with the ladder. A loud thud and then a crash are heard as the ladder falls on top of him. Muttering, he attempts to lift the ladder off and stand up, but his foot catches on one of the rungs, and he falls forward, slamming his face into the side of the pit. Muttering again, he just lays there for a moment, cross-eyed, trying to blow a small clump of dirt off his nose. He gets up slowly to check out his situation. Very carefully he sets the ladder against the side of the pit and pushes it gently to be sure it is safe. Carefully, he begins to climb. Looking up, he sees Sparky holding the ladder steady.

Reaching safety at the top, Jenks looks at Sparky with a sheepish grin as another chunk of dirt falls from his bushy unibrow and bounces off his nose. Sparky just groans and walks away, shaking his head as he passes by Hook, who has been watching this unfolding fiasco with a self-sadistic curiosity.

"Why do I subject myself to the antics of this dumb, slimy parasite?"

Chapter 43

Rascal Bait

It is late evening. The pirates are all tired and soiled from the digging, but no one complains for fear of provoking Hook's wrath. Hook orders the pirate Goose and the smaller pirate Gyps, "I want you two to sneak over to where those annoying kids are."

Gyps is a bit surprised. "Where the Rascals are?"

"Yes, you heard me. You will bring me back two of the smaller boys."

Gyps is astonished at this bizarre request. "Bring back what?"

Hook's annoyance increases. "Is there an echo? Just shut up and listen. Sneak over there, watch until they're alone, away from the others, then snatch 'em up and bring 'em back to me. Do you understand?"

"Snatch 'em up? Bring 'em back to you? Ain't that dangerous, Cap'n? That is two days' journey."

Hook glares at him as he raises his sword. "You heard me! Just do it, or the sword! Now take a net, you imbeciles, sacks and some twine. And here, leave this note."

The pirates glance at the note. Hook has signed his name in large block letters, JAMES HOOK. He leans forward, places himself face-to-face with them, and menacingly taps his hook with his sword. "Are you still here?"

The scared pirates back away. "Okay, okay! We're going!"

* * * *

After a long tramp through the island jungle and camping overnight, Goose and Gyps make their way to the other side of the island where the Rascals live. The pirates sneak around and position themselves where they can see the goings-on without being seen.

After a while, Gyps sees two smaller boys play as they walk. "Look, them are there."

The pirates watch, and follow Sneezer and PJ's as they play and walk further away from the rest. The pirates listen when the boys stop to talk under a tree. PJ's is talking about Peter. "Neverland is fun, but it would be so much funner with Peter."

Sneezer agrees. "I think it's funnerest if Peter's here."

"Funnerest?" Goose wonders out loud. "What does that mean?"

Gyps shakes his head. "Them sure are dumb kids, ain't them?"

A moment later, a net drops over the boys. They struggle but can't get loose. The pirates quickly gag and shove the boys into large burlap sacks and tie them tightly shut with twine. Goose then tacks Hook's note on the tree. "Remember, we have to make a trail they can follow, like Hook said." The note tells the other Rascals not to follow them. Of course, this is Hook's ingenious plan—to tell them not to follow, so they will.

The boys kick and thrash around in the sacks, throwing the pirates off balance as they toss the sacks over their shoulders. Gyps nearly falls to the ground from all of the thrashing around. Growling, he warns, "Stop yer thrashin', or you'll get the blade."

Chapter 44

Gone Missing

Ambo and Hawkins notice that Sneezer and PJ's are nowhere in sight. Ambo shouts to the others, "Has anyone seen PJ's or Sneezer?" They all start looking around for the two boys.

Tain laughs. "Maybe they're playing a trick on us."

Aky grins from ear to ear. "It's another great game! Hide and Seek! Let's go! It's Hide and Seek!"

Hearing the yelling and laughter, Tinker Bell peeks out and sees the four of them looking under and around bushes here, there and everywhere. The game is just too much for her to resist, so now, back to her happy self, she joins in. The Rascals are all spread out farther from the treehouse than usual. Everyone is wondering where the youngsters might be hiding.

Whippy seems a bit uneasy. "PJ's and Sneezer have never hidden this far out before."

Tinker Bell agrees. "You're absolutely right, and there is something not right about this. You and the others go back to the treehouse. I'll check things a little further out and meet you back there."

They all begin to make their way back home while Tinker Bell scours the ground below for any sign of the kids. Suddenly, she spots a piece of paper stuck to a tree. Flying down to it as fast as she can, she realizes it's a note. "What's a note doing all the way out here? Who would even think to leave a note here? Are the boys trying to trick us?" She pulls the note off the tree, reads it, and glows red with rage when she sees it was signed by Hook.

Furious, she begins to spin around, flying up and down with such great energy that the windy aftermath causes the trees and vegetation to bend in the path of her whirlwind of rage. She looks at the note again and reddens even more. "Hook! How can this be Hook? It can't be, but this is his signature. He won't get away with this."

Tain and the others observe a red streak coming in from high above the trees. "What the hey is that?" It is soon obvious as Tinker Bell returns, landing on the table. They approach her cautiously; they have never seen her so angry. "What is it? What's wrong?"

Tinker Bell, glowing a bit less, hands the note to Whippy. "This is what's wrong."

Whippy reads the note aloud. "Hook signed this note, so he's behind it?"

Hawkins points at him. "But you know Hook is dead!"

Whippy shakes his head. "I know, but this could really be his signature."

Tinker Bell, now back to her normal glow, takes charge. "That is Hook's signature. Let's get organized." She mutters, "After all this time, how can this be Hook?"

They have a short group meeting. The plan is to send a search party to find PJ's and Sneezer. The others will stay to watch their home, in case whoever is behind this plot might be planning more trouble for them. Tootles speaks up boldly. "Great plan. I'll stay here and keep a watchful eye with the rest."

Crane raises his hand. "I'll lead the search party. Who else is going with me?"

Kilowatts and Pinner step forward. "We'll go."

Tinker Bell impatiently darts back-and-forth above their heads as she waits for them to put on their war-paint and gather together a few supplies.

Chapter 45

The Search Begins

The three Rascals and Tinker Bell start to follow the trail left by Goose and Gyps. It leads them through the forest and into the swamp. Tinker Bell speaks up. "There are some things in the swamps we don't want to meet up with. Keep your eyes open."

This makes the kids a little nervous as they keep an eye out. They hear growls and splashing in the mud every now and then, as if something is following them.

After a long, slow trek through the swamp, they are covered with mud. Kilowatts checks out the trail ahead. "Sure looks like we'll be going over the mountain."

Tinker Bell, flying back-and-forth, thinks aloud, "We may find more trouble than we can handle alone."

Crane hears her. "I wish Peter were here, especially if we find big trouble."

"What would Peter want me to do? What should I do? Should I stay or go?" She is a little anxious about her decision, unsure if it's the right one. "I will go back and help protect our home."

Pinner is frustrated and tired. "Peter won't ever come back here. He has been gone so long he has forgotten."

Remembering Peter's last adventure in Neverland, Crane is more confident. "It's been a long time, but Peter will come back."

Kilowatts is also confident. "He'll be back, you'll see."

Pinner sighs deeply. "I hope you're right."

Tinker Bell flies back to the Rascals' home. All are worried, including her. Ambo notices she isn't her usual self, the way she repeats the words 'stay or go' over and over.

"Tinker Bell, are you okay? You're acting, well, kinda funny. Wanna talk?"

Tinker Bell is a bit short with Ambo. "Nothing to talk about."

Hawkins is close enough to hear the tone of her voice. "What's wrong?"

Tinker Bell raises one eyebrow and says with even more attitude, "Nothing to talk about."

Hawkins is taken aback by Tinker Bell's impatience. "Well, okay, then, if you don't want to share, but we are all worried too, you know!"

Tinker Bell backs off a bit, "I know, I know, I was thinking that if I go get Peter and bring him back, he would surely know how to deal with anything that might happen. No trouble is too big for Peter! I will have to find where he lives."

Hawkins echoes her fisted stance. "You're right! Peter will rip their lip!"

Ambo chuckles, amused at Hawkins. "Yes, he will!"

Tinker Bell knows everyone would feel safer if she waited a little longer. She is very small but extremely powerful. "I'll go if we don't hear anything soon."

Chapter 46

Pitiful in the Pit

After a long, tiring journey through swamps, forest, and snow on the mountain, the boys make their way into the jungle, staying hot on the trail to find the kidnapped Rascals. Bangarangatang keeps a watchful eye from high up in the trees as the boys follow the clues. Up ahead they see a small clearing. The monkey screeches and jumps on a limb above their heads as he points ahead. The boys realize he is warning them about something. They approach the clearing cautiously.

Kilowatts sees them first. "There they are!"

PJ's and Sneezer are tied to a tree with gags over their mouths. Forgetting about being careful, Pinner runs toward them, yelling, "We found them!"

The others are close behind—too close. Quick as a wink they all drop out of sight. A loud thud is heard as they hit the bottom of the pit. Bangarangatang shakes his head, puts his fingers over his eyes, bares his teeth, and groans. After all, he did try to warn them.

Pinner, Kilowatts, and Crane are pretty well shaken up from the unexpected fall. Hook's plan, well executed, excites his very being. He fiendishly smiles as he nears the edge of the pit and hears the groans. The boys get up one by one, brush themselves off, and look around, trying to evaluate their situation as Hook peers over them at the edge of the pit with his band of pirates dutifully at his sides.

"Hello, boys. Are you cozy?"

Crane groans in anguish as he points up. Stunned at the sight of Hook, the boys are horrified and shriek out in unison, "It's Hook!"

Kilowatts looks up and rubs his eyes. "It can't be. The croc ate him. Is it a ghost?"

"Ah, yes! Indeed, it is I, Hook. Have you missed me?"

Pinner hardly believes what he is seeing. "But you're supposed to be dead!"

Hook rubs his chin. "Mmmmm, is that a fact? Seems I forgot, so I'm not." Arrogantly and with great abandon, he continues, "You seem to forget, I am Neverland!"

"What kind of game are you playing?" Crane angrily grumbles.

"Playing? What a novel idea! Let's play a great game."

"Game?" the three boys reply in unison.

No longer amused, Hook pulls his sword and points it down into the pit. "Oh, yes, and the name of this great game is Cap-tured!"

Delighted by Hook's sense of perverse humor, the pirates begin to chant, "Hook is back! Hook is back!"

Chapter 47

Digestin' the Suggestion

All are gathered around the long table, including Tall Tree and Brown Cow. All are worried, including Goatee, who senses something is wrong.

Tinker Bell stands in the middle of the table. "It's been too long. The boys haven't come back. Something is very wrong."

Tootles, wise in his age, says, "Aye, Tinker Bell, that's right, something's not right. They should have been back with the little ones by now."

Tinker Bell looks around at each one. "Any suggestions?"

"We could send out the two-girl scouting party," Tootles says. "They are sneaky."

Silence falls on the group. Okydoky stands up. "Let's us be digestin' this suggestion, but this might be the right right. We have to do something."

Whippy and Big C offer to go, but Ambo jumps up and looks over at Hawkins, "We'll go! Just let those pirates try something! I'll rip their lip! Right, Hawkins?"

Hawkins claps her hands. "I think it is the right right, too, BANGARANG!"

Big C does not agree. "This is too dangerous for girls."

Ambo jumps up in front of Big C and pulls her sword. "Want to try me?"

Big C backs away. "No, no!" He contemplates her idea. "You would be a great asset to our scouting party."

Ambo lowers her sword. "Thought you'd see it my way, but there is no 'our,' just me and Hawkins."

Okydoky gets into the mix. "After digestin' the suggestion, I be surely wantin' to go too, but maybe the girls have a point. They be more sneakierest and lots quieterest!"

Tinker Bell warns the girls, "Be very careful. We don't know what's happened to them. If Hook is really alive, it could be really big and tricky trouble."

Hawkins agrees. "We won't do anything but scout 'em out and return with the information."

Ambo and Hawkins pack some food and water for the day, as well as a slingshot and swords, in case they run into any unforeseen trouble along the way. As they get ready to go, Goatee starts sniffing around the food. Hawkins tries to shoo him away, but he keeps bumping her leg with his head. Ambo tries to lead him, but he keeps pulling her back.

Thinking he just wants the food, Hawkins says, "Goatee, you can't have it. This is for our trip."

The goat gets up on his hind legs and shakes his head. His front hooves reach up as he paws like a cat, wanting to jump into a lap. Hawkins tilts her head to one side and looks at the eager goat. "Goatee, want to go too?"

He responds by jumping up and down.

"Well, I guess Goatee wants to go, too."

Ambo isn't really sure if the animal should go. "He might get lost, or something might happen to him."

Hawkins, though thinks it's cute. "Oh, what harm could it do? Besides, he'll probably get bored after we get out there and just come back here."

"I guess so. Okay, Goatee goes."

Chapter 48

Bangarangatang Knows

Through the forest and swamp, over the mountain, and after camping for the night, the girls and the goat arrive next morning at the jungle, which seems very quiet and strange. A breeze swishes through, and twigs and bark fall from the trees. At first the girls think it's just the breeze blowing the debris loose from the branches. But more twigs fall, and then a coconut drops right in front of them. They look up to see Bangarangatang jumping from branch to branch, screeching at the top of his lungs.

Hawkins laughs at his antics. "What's all that monkeying around, you silly monkey?"

Bangarangatang drops down out of the tree in front of them, screeching and hurling dirt and leaves in the air. Ambo watches him intently. "I think he's trying to tell us something."

Goatee runs toward the monkey as if to butt him. Hawkins reaches out to grab the goat but isn't quick enough. "No! Goatee, no!" The goat reaches the monkey but doesn't butt him. They just sniff at each other's noses, as if communicating. Abruptly, Goatee turns and begins to bump the girls to turn them back. Bangarangatang became even more animated, flinging more dirt and leaves at them.

Hawkins, who knows Goatee best, says, "I think he's trying to tell us something. Maybe he doesn't want us to go any further." (Indeed, Bangarangatang and Goatee tried their best to let the girls know that was precisely the case.) Hawkins slowly walks a little ways farther toward a clearing. Bangarangatang sees her and runs after her, grabbing her leg to pull her back. "I know, I know, you don't want me to go any further."

Ambo and Goatee catch up. Ambo crouches down so as not to be seen and looks through the large jungle leaves at the edge of the clearing. Hawkins creeps up and peeks, too. They both see the same thing: PJ's and Sneezer tied to a tree.

"This sure looks like a trap to me, Hawkins," Ambo says.

Bangarangatang pulls Hawkins' leg harder. Goatee cuts in front of Ambo, pushing her back. The girls get the message loud and clear: go no further. With that they sneak away and head back home. Bangarangatang tags along with them, riding atop the goat.

The sun is beginning to set, so they find a safe place to rest until morning. Ambo reflects on how Goatee and the monkey knew. "They sure did a good job of letting us know there was trouble ahead."

Hawkins agrees. "They're smarter than they look. But I never knew a goat could talk monkey."

Bangarangatang jumps off Goatee, grabs him by his goatee, and screeches out, "Baaaaaaah!" The girls laugh at the animal antics and roll on the ground. Ambo speaks up. "Actually, this is a very serious problem. Let's settle down for the night and think about what we can do. We have an early start in the morning."

<h1 style="text-align:center">Chapter 49</h1>

<h1 style="text-align:center">The Great Scary April</h1>

Early the next morning, the girls, Goatee, and Bangarangatang head out over the mountain and down into the forest. Ambo and Hawkins discuss strategies for rescuing the boys. Ambo remembers how Big C objected to the girls going. "Big C was sure full of it when he felt we couldn't track the boys, huh, Hawkins?"

But Hawkins is enchanted by the beauty of the forest. "How lovely Neverland is."

Ambo looks up at the foliage and flowers and nods in agreement. "So, sooo much better than the orphanage and cold, cold snow. Seems like a bad dream from long ago."

Hawkins looks over at Ambo. "I think it was long ago, and a bad dream."

At that moment, a loud, menacing roar somewhere on the trail ahead pierces the quiet serenity of the morning. They hear loud thuds, like someone stomping, and it is getting closer. Once again, another roar shakes them to the core.

"What do we do, Ambo?"

Ambo looks down at Hawkins. "Don't know yet."

The girls proceed cautiously and are startled by the sudden appearance of a huge gorilla, whose teeth glisten in the morning sun. They freeze in their tracks, realizing the danger, as they size up this monster of an ape. Another great roar spews from its mouth as saliva drips down its face. Ambo slowly pulls out her sword, backs up, trips over a fallen branch, and loses her balance as her sword falls to the ground. She quickly picks it up, but Hawkins jumps in front of her and shouts in her loudest voice, "Get back, you big ape, or I'll rip your lip!"

The ape tilts her head, curious about this little screechy voice, and shakes her finger at Hawkins as if to say, No, no, little girl, this is how you roar. She opens her large mouth really wide and lets out such a great roar that the leaves and branches tremble. Standing at full height, the mighty ape begins to pound her chest.

Hawkins reconsiders her lip-ripping proposal. "Well, maybe not."

Bangarangatang, screeching loudly, drops from the tree onto the gorilla's head and covers her eyes with his little monkey paws. Goatee, not missing a beat, lowers his head, charges, and jumps up right into the gorilla's belly. Ambo points her sword at the ape. Oddly, this huge monster sits down on the path in front of them and groans.

As the girls watch in amazement, the gorilla puts her hand over a very swollen cheek and whimpers. Bangarangatang, still on her head, crawls down her face and, surprisingly, opens the giant creature's mouth. Looking inside, the monkey sees the ape's problem. Screeching and pointing, he summons the girls, who creep closer to the gorilla cautiously.

Ambo gets close enough to poke her head almost into the ape's mouth. "Wow, there's a big old thorn in the gum here. It must hurt like heck."

Hawkins remembers a story she heard about a gorilla. "Wait a minute, this must be April, the gorilla from a story I once heard. I never thought it was true, but here you are!”

The gorilla nods her head while holding her cheek.

Ambo is still cautious. “Well, this really is April! We have to help her and get that thorn out. Oh, boy! You ready, April?”

The great ape nods again.

Working together, Ambo holds April’s mouth wide open as Hawkins grabs the thorn and yanks it out. April feels the relief and grins widely, holding out her huge hand to say thanks. The girls reach up to give the great ape’s hand a reassuring pat. Without a wink, April grabs up both girls in a great big gorilla bear-hug, then gently puts them down and disappears into the forest. Hawkins, trying to catch her breath, looks over at Ambo, who has her hands on her knees. Trying to catch her breath as well, Ambo says, “I’m glad this was a happy hug.”

Goatee takes the lead on the trail. The girls follow as they watch Bangarangatang climb up into the trees. Looking down, he chatters at them to say good-bye and disappears into the treetops.

Hawkins looks up at Ambo. “Wow, now that was sure a great adventure!”

Chapter 50

April Stories Don't Fly

The girls arrive back at the treehouse, where Big C is giving orders. "We'll take our slingshots and swords in case we run into any trouble."

"That's a good idea," Puff agrees.

"But how will we know you're all okay?" Tootles asks.

Big C puts his hand over his heart. "We'll get word back to you, I promise."

Hawkins tries to get a word in to share the adventure she and Ambo just experienced. "There was this huge, really huge gorilla, and—" She is cut off as Big C continues to organize the search party.

Ambo shakes her head. "Big C, don't you even want to know what happened to us and what we found out?"

Big C is acting all busy, and even a little annoyed. "Okay, okay, what is it?"

Ambo puts her hands on her hips. "Why don't you just sit down a minute and listen?"

Big C grunts, "Go ahead, let's hear it."

Disliking Big C's attitude, Hawkins gets up in his face, "And shut up, or I'll rip your lip!"

At this point Big C has no choice but to sit down, keep quiet, and listen to the girls, who begin by sharing their sight of Sneezer and PJ's tied to a tree. Big C smirks in disbelief. "Well, if you saw them tied to a tree, why didn't you just untie them and bring them back with you?"

"How about you shut up and let us finish what we have to say?" pipes up Ambo, also frustrated with Big C's attitude. "They were tied to this tree, but when we started over to rescue them, Bangarangatang and Goatee wouldn't let us go any further and kept us back in the jungle."

"We can lead you to exactly where we were, but you won't have any problems with the giant gorilla," Hawkins adds. "We took care of that already."

Big C shakes his head and raises one eyebrow. "Are you trying to tell me that two girls, a mindless monkey and a goofy goat handled a giant gorilla? Yeah, right! We have to get going, or it'll be too dark to even get going."

"We can lead you there."

"No, you girls stay here. The trail should be easy enough to follow. After all, you two found the tree where the boys were tied up."

Hawkins crosses her arms and puts a frown on her face. "I should've ripped his lip anyway! Oh, by the way, if you run into April, tell her we say hello."

"Well, I guess our adventure will just have to wait until they hopefully get back with the boys." Ambo sits down with her head in her hands.

Chapter 51

Ambo's Imagination

Searching along the easy-to-follow path, Big C, Whippy and Puff trudge through the forest and over the mountain, as did the girls. The day has ended, and the evening shadows are beginning to creep over the swamp. The boys decide it would be best to make camp and continue on their trek in the morning at first light.

After a restless night, the three searchers are awakened by the loud snappings of branches and the thuds of heavy footsteps nearing their camp. The footfalls stop as a hideous roar shakes the trees. The boys scramble to pick up their slingshots, take aim, and slowly inch their way in the direction of the roar. The three of them make it only a few feet when a much closer roar frightens them into retreat in three different directions. After the initial shock, they regroup on the trail a few minutes later.

Whippy is still shaking. "What creature could have made that horrible roar? Maybe it was Ambo's imagination!"

Big C is scared as well. "Yeah, and for the first time in my life I really don't want to know. Let's go."

Continuing their search for the missing boys, they follow the trail into the jungle to the other side of the island. Bangarangatang has been following and watching them from high up in the trees. Now they are very close to the same opening in which the girls saw PJ's and Sneezer tied up. The monkey jumps down in front of them and tries to warn them not to go any further. At that moment Puff sees the boys tied to a tree with gags over their mouths and yells out, "There they are!"

Ignoring the monkey, the three boys run toward PJ's and Sneezer and are suddenly engulfed in the pirates' pit. Bangarangatang, screeching wildly, darts back into the trees.

Shaken up by the deep fall, Big C, Whippy and Puff get up one by one, brush themselves off, and look around to evaluate their situation. "Is everyone okay?" Puff asks his comrades. "Is anyone hurt?"

Whippy brushes himself off and rubs his face. "No, we're okay, but what happened? How did we get into this mess?"

"Well, duh, we fell into a hole." Puff points at Big C. "You...you wouldn't listen to the girls, the goat, or the monkey. I guess they're smarter than you."

Big C is fumbling to find something to say. "But, if I had, it wasn't."

"Shut up, C!" snap the other two.

"Never mind what happened—how do we get out of this mess?" Whippy groans while brushing the dirt off of his face and hair.

PEACE IN NEVERLAND

THINK HAPPY THOUGHTS!

A SECRET PLACE

AMBO

TAIN

BIG C

SMEE

HOOK

Chapter 52

'I Am Quite Back'

The boys hear laughter and noise above them. Looking up from the bottom of the pit, they see Hook and his band of pirates around the edge. Hook laughs loudly, "You don't get out of it. Ahhhh, this is just too good."

Whippy is shocked, surprised, and almost speechless. "It's Hooook!"

Big C, normally never at a loss for words, looks up and rubs his chin. "It is scientifically impossible to come back from the dead. Therefore, this cannot be. It just can't be." Pointing up at Hook, Big C tries to get a handle on this sudden event. "But you're supposed to be dead!"

Hook rubs his chin in a like manner. "Yes, as a matter of fact that is exactly what they tell me." He turns to his motley crew and grins from ear to ear. "Hmmm, dead, not dead, back, not back, it's all a croc."

The pirates delight in Hook's perverted humor. Looking down at the boys, he says, "It is so amusin' to see the confusion in your eyes." He grins and reiterates his position: "I assure you, I am quite back."

Puff collects his thoughts. "Untie the boys from that tree?"

Hook responds softly, "Ah, yes, my pit needs the boys for bait. Sorry, it's Bangarang boys. Ha-haaaa!"

Smee turns to the other pirates and shouts, "BANGARANG!" The pirates laugh and mock the boys in unison, "BANG, BANG, BANGARANG,

BANGARANG!"

No longer amused, Hook sternly orders his men, "Okay, you gathering guppies, get this lot out of the pit. Tie 'em up and move 'em down the trail with the other three. We'll just leave the two tied to the tree. Great bait, they are."

PJ's and Sneezer shake their heads and groan. The pirates laugh. "They'll get their water and food," Hook says. "Don't want them passing before we get our prize! Har!"

"What is the prize?" Puff asks.

Hook spins and points down at him. "The Pan."

The monkey watches from the trees as the pirates lower a ladder into the pit. Puff grabs it, twisting and turning it as the first pirate starts down. The pirate loses his grip and falls in. Another pirate is already coming down, and another behind him. Puff reaches for his sword, but too late. The first pirate grabs Big C, turns him around and puts a knife to his throat. "Try anything, and I'll slit your throat ear to ear."

The other pirates are now on the floor of the pit. They quickly edge the boys to the ladder and thrust the tips of their swords in their faces. "Up the ladder, laddie!"

Whippy feels the sword poke him on the backside. "We get the point, you plundering parasite pirate!"

Once out of the pit, the pirates tie the boys' hands, raise a long pole, and order them, "Get yer hands in the air." Whippy, Puff, and Big C raise their tied hands up, and the pirates thread the pole through the ropes. The boys lift their feet and squirm around in an effort to knock the pirates off balance and maybe have a chance to escape, but the pirate's shoulders are stronger than they thought.

* * * *

It is late afternoon. Whippy, Puff, and Big C are now on their way down the trail, hands roped and poled, led on by Hook and the pirates. They all trudge along to the area where the other pirates are holding Kilowatts, Pinner, and Crane. Hook motions for the two groups of boys to be brought together. "Line 'em up, and tie 'em proper!"

The boys are tied three feet apart on a long, heavy rope, resembling a centipede, as the pirates chant the "Hook is back" tune while the entire entourage of buccaneers and boys marches down the trail. Hook twists his hook to the beat of the chant and leads the parade on the long journey back to the dock and onto his ship.

Jenks and Sparky bring up the rear, as usual. Sparky looks up as Bangarangatang harasses him by jumping around, pointing and screeching at him. "Monkey doomed." Jenks jokes, "Monkey see, monkey doomed." He starts laughing almost as much as the monkey does. Sparky glares at him in a way that makes Jenks stop laughing. Jenks grins sheepishly, showing his snaggle teeth. "Just makin' fun."

* * * *

It is late evening. The boys are imprisoned in the bowels of the ship, unable to see the array of light across the water. The moon is rising, and the diminishing sunlight dances with the moonlight. Multi-colored beams shimmer over the water, blending moon and sun colors, creating a mystical end to yet another day in Neverland.

The pirates are on the deck, resting, sharpening knives and swords, or playing shell games. Many are drinking rum and eating grub as they indulge in pirate-type conversation, laughing as they talk about the latest captives and, of course, Jenks' antics while falling into the pit. It seems to be a lazy, quiet evening for the pirates on Hook's ship—at least for the moment.

JENKS

Chapter 53

'Better Than a Poke in the Stick'

Hook steps out of his quarters onto the upper deck to look over his ship and crew. Annoyed at their laziness and lack of discipline, he bellows, "Get busy, you pitiful, pathetic lot of pungent pirates, and hoist the sails! You all know what to do, and practice makes perfect!"

The pirates muster to their positions and begin the drill.

Hook knows his new captives will bring Peter to the rescue, but that there will be no rescue, as Peter is sure to fall into Hook's trap, too. "Won't be long now! We'll have him soon and then off to Davy Jones' locker. There's no escape, Peter Pan! I hate, I hate, I hate Peter Pan!"

The crew has settled in, each man at his post. The murmur of softly sung pirate songs fills the air. Hook is pleased as he looks over the deck; all the men know their duties. Then he sees Jenks just standing there, watching it all. Hook leans over the deck, growing angry as he observes Jenks for several minutes. Slowly, Hook descends the steps, but Jenks is unaware. Down the steps and onto the deck, Hook quietly approaches Jenks, staring at him with one eye, like a crow eyeing a sparkling gem. Jenks suddenly realizes he's not alone, gasps as Hook approaches, and shrinks down in fear.

The one eye seems to get larger as Hook lays his sword between Jenks' eyes. "That meant you, matey! Get to, or I'll cut you from stem to stern."

Jenks looks cross-eyed at the sword but doesn't move a muscle. "Aye, Cap'n meant me, too. I'll be gettin' to. Better'n a poke in the stick with a sharp eye, Cap'n."

Hook pulls back his sword. "I am astounded. I have never heard such sub-intellectual gibberish from such a fool."

Relieved the sword is no longer between his eyes, Jenks displays his sheepish, snaggle-toothed grin.

Not amused by Jenks' attempt at humor, Hook lifts his sword to take a swing. "Better than a poke in the eye with a sharp stick, you mumbling, bumbling idiot."

Jenks takes off like a bullet. Hook turns and walks off in disgust. Still running, Jenks doesn't notice the blocking rope right in front of him until his foot is caught in it and he is hoisted up. Hanging and swinging upside down by the one foot, he calls for help, but no one can hear him over the singing. "P'leeeze, someone get me down! Helllllp!"

A while later, Jenks is still hanging in the air. All is quiet on deck, since everyone has turned in for the night.

A short while later, Sparky, just coming up from down below, walks the deck. The full moon casts eerie shadows on the deck, making him just a bit nervous. He hears something and looks around. Hearing it again, he gets a little jumpy. He turns a corner, jumps back and lets out a shout, as if he has just seen a ghost.

Jenks, still hanging, emits a blood-curdling scream, awakened and scared by Sparky's yell. Jenks had fallen asleep; the noise Sparky heard was Jenks' snoring.

Calming himself, Sparky gets Jenks down. "Hung up, uuhhrrrrr?"

Jenks voice is a little shaky. "Thanks, Sparky… Oh, my head."

Chapter 54

Together Again

Back at the treehouse, Tinker Bell gathers everyone for a meeting, including Tootles, Hawkins, Ambo, Tall Tree, Brown Cow, Tain, Okydoky and Aky. "Something's wrong," she says, "and I'm going back to find Peter!"

Tootles is worried. "Okay, Tinker Bell, I'll see to things here, and you find 'im quick." He explains to her where Peter lives. Everyone agrees that the only thing to do now is to find Peter and bring him back. This venture is just too big for them to handle alone.

Tinker Bell is ready to go. All wave and wish her a safe journey as she takes off into the clouds with a flash of rainbow colors and flies completely out of sight.

After a long flight, Tinker Bell heads down through the clouds to begin her search for Peter. "I'm almost positive Peter's house is somewhere nearby." She veers north for a bit, then south, and then spots a house that looks familiar. "There it is! I knew I was in the right area." She darts down and peers into the windows. No one is there. All she sees are sheets on the furniture, and everything is locked up. Landing on the branch of a nearby tree, she ponders, "Now, where could they have gone?"

Just then, the next-door neighbors, George and Ethel, approach their mailbox. Ethel reaches in to get their mail and sighs, "Isn't it wonderful that young people can afford a trip to England for the whole family?"

George agrees. "Yup, it sure is, but wasn't it Scotland?"

Ethel shakes her head and smiles. "Oh, George, let's go get our lunch."

When Tinker Bell hears this, she knows exactly where Peter went. "Wendy's house, of course!" Setting her course for England, she soars off, planning to arrive around sunset.

*   *   *   *

Tinker Bell lands atop a statue of a boy playing the flute in Wendy's garden. Looking around, she flies up to the second-floor balcony and gazes through the French windows but doesn't see anything. Sitting dejectedly on the balcony railing with her head in her hands and wings drooping, she cries, "Isn't anyone home?"

After a long while, she looks up to see the sun now gone and a full moon and starry sky lighting up the heavens. She stares at the brightest star on the right—Neverland. As if it can hear her, it twinkles brightly. She responds, "We will be back, me and Peter."

Thinking about returning with Peter brightens her glow and flitters her wings. Suddenly she hears voices from the first floor and flies down to the large bay window in the family room, but the blinds are closed. "Maybe I didn't hear any voices. Maybe I'm too anxious. I have to quit being so impatient." Back up on the balcony railing, her soft glow illuminates the spot where her tiny figure rests. Her back is to the window, her hands are on the rail, and her legs hang over the balcony as she gazes up at the stars.

Peter, Trish, Wendy, and Poppy are indeed in the family room, chatting and enjoying tea and crumpets. Peter stands up. "Trish, I think I'll go up and check on the kids."

Trish notices Peter's anxiety. "But you just checked on them twenty minutes ago."

Peter nods his head. "I know, but it'll only take a minute."

"Peter, Hook is dead, they're safe, and we are going to bed."

Peter nods again but starts upstairs.

*   *   *   *

The glow from the nightlights above the beds casts a shadow over the murals on the wall. The shadows seem to bring life to the figures painted there. Peter is mesmerized by the illusion, and it brings back memories of Hook. "I hate Hook," he mutters.

As Peter bends over the children's beds to check on them, his eye catches a glimpse of another soft glow. He thinks it is just a reflection in the window. Once satisfied that the children are fine, he walks to their door. Reaching for the knob, he realizes the third glow is not a reflection. He turns toward the French window and cautiously makes his way toward it. He hesitates, then reaches out to open it. All at once, a bright flash of light flies past him into the room. He jumps back, losing his balance, and falls into the rocking chair. The noise is fortunately not loud enough to awaken the children.

Peter immediately realizes it is Tinker Bell, flying at super speed all around the room. "Tinker Bell, what a surprise! Glad to see you, but what are you doing here?"

She is so fired up she can hardly talk. Her glow is so bright it lights up the room. "Hook has them. He's taken some of our Rascals. We need you. Neverland needs you."

Peter squints against her brightness. "Tinker Bell, calm down. You're so on fire, and your light will wake up the kids."

"Did you hear me?"

"What are you talking about? Hook is dead!"

Tinker Bell is shocked. "Peter, you're grown up! Is that you?"

"Yes, Tinker Bell, it's me. I have a family now."

Her mind is racing. "A family?"

"What did you say about Hook not being dead? He is dead."

"No, no, he's not! I don't know how, but he is back. We have to go right now!" She grabs Peter by the shirt and pulls him toward the balcony.

"This can't be! Hook is gone!"

Tinker Bell is getting more frantic. "Peter, it's true! Hook is back."

Peter looks back at the children. They are still asleep. He rubs his face in disbelief. "You mean—Oh, no, not again!"

Tinker Bell tugs harder at his shirt. "Yes, it's true! We can't wait! We have to go right now!"

Peter stands firm. "I hate Hook!"

"We all hate Hook! Now let's get going!"

Peter knows his responsibility to his wife and children, but he is also aware of his great love for Neverland and the Rascals. He walks in circles, mumbling to himself, trying to sort out the situation in his mind.

Tinker Bell is frustrated with his stalling. "Peter, we have to go now, right now!"

Peter hesitates before leaving the room. "I know I have to go back, but I have to talk with Trish first."

Tinker Bell, trying to be patient and understanding, flies up atop one of the nightlights to wait for his return. "Hurry, Peter."

Chapter 55

'I Wish it Was the Bathroom'

Trish appears to be asleep when Peter enters their bedroom. He walks to her bedside and gently touches her on the shoulder. "Trish, are you awake? I have to go now. It can't wait."

Trish is still half asleep. "If you have to go, it hasn't moved. It's still down the hall."

"No, Trish, not that. I've got to go. It isn't over yet. They need me."

Trish replies sleepily, "What are you talking about? Peter, have you been drinking? What isn't over?"

Peter looks up at the ceiling. He doesn't want to alarm her. "Tinker Bell is upstairs, and Hook is alive!"

Trish opens her eyes. "Tinker Bell upstairs? Hook is alive? Now I know you've been drinking. What are you babbling about?"

Trying to calm himself, Peter whispers, "It was supposed to be over, but somehow, some way, Hook is back from the dead!"

"Peter, you're scaring me. Are you having a bad dream?"

"I don't mean to frighten you, but listen to me, Trish. Hook is back. Somehow he is alive. It's not over, and he's taken some of the Neverland Rascals."

Trish sits up. "I don't understand how this has happened, but I do know you haven't been yourself all this time… Who are the Neverland Rascals?"

Peter hugs her gently and kisses her on the forehead. "I have no choice. I must go."

"Yes, Peter, I understand, you must go. That pure hatred toward Hook has been brewing up in you for a long time, and now it is even more justified."

Peter is relieved. "Yes, Trish, and I have to end it once and for all, or I'll never be free of it."

Trish stands up, speaking softly, "You must have felt deep down that it wasn't over. It's been making you crazy. I do understand, but who are the Neverland Rascals?"

Peter holds her close and kisses her. "Thank you, even more than you know. I'll explain about the Rascals later." He turns away, but Trish grabs his hand and stops him. "Go. Finish it and be done with your hatred once and for all."

Still holding her hand, he pulls her close and whispers, "Tell the kids how much I love them, and that I'll be back soon."

He leaves the room. Trish sits back down on the bed, murmuring, "I wish it was the bathroom!"

*　*　*　*

The moon shines through the stained-glass window at the top of the stairway. Peter notices its eerie glow and pauses for a moment, staring at the window, then quickly ascends the stairs, his mind racing with thoughts of hatred toward Hook. Stopping near the top, he doubles his fist in anger. "This time it will be finished!"

He re-enters the children's room. They are still sleeping peacefully. He whispers, "I love you more than you know, and I promise I'll be back soon."

Tinker Bell, annoyed by the delay, flies down in front of Peter's nose, making him look cross-eyed. "Aren't you ready yet?"

Without a word he steps out on the balcony, and Tinker Bell sprinkles him with fairy dust. "I'm looking forward to taking Hook out for good," he declares.

They fly through the night sky. Their silhouettes appear over the rooftops and against the full moon. Then they disappear into the heavens.

Chapter 56

Peter to the Rescue

Tinker Bell and Peter fly through the billows of rainbow dust above Neverland. As they break through the barrier flash and descend through the clouds, Peter notices he has changed. He stops and looks at his hands and feet. "I'm a kid again! Wow! I'll have to do something about my clothes. They're falling off."

Tinker Bell snickers and looks over at Peter with great enthusiasm and a big smile. "You are really, really back, for sure. I think you are Neverland! Together again, Peter, for another great adventure?"

In unison they holler, "BANGARANG!"

It is morning in Neverland. The sun is coming up over the horizon, casting its rays through the boughs and branches of the treehouse. Peter takes a deep breath and looks all around. "Neverland is my first and forever home."

* * * *

Tall Tree and Brown Cow are sleeping beside a smoldering campfire. Tootles is standing next to the big tree, rubbing his eyes and yawning. Stretching his arms, he sees Peter and Tinker Bell flying down from the clouds. He runs over to the campfire and tries to wake up the natives. In his excitement he inadvertently puts his foot in the hot ashes. In his attempt to get it out, he accidentally puts the other foot down there as well. He hops back-and-forth, one foot to the other, and whoops out in pain, "Ouch! Ouch! That really hurts!"

His yelling awakens the natives. Tall Tree pokes Brown Cow and points at Tootles. "Him think him doing rain dance."

Brown Cow watches Tootles cavort amid the ashes. "Ugh, him do funny dance!"

Tootles cried out in pain, "I'm not dancing! The bottoms of my feet are burning!"

Tall Tree begins to laugh. "You got hot feet."

Brown Cow is totally disinterested. "Why not dance out of ashes?"

Tootles dances out of the hot ashes, excitedly points toward the spot where Peter and Tinker Bell have landed, and shouts, "Tinker Bell is back! And Peter's with her!"

The ruckus awakens the rest of the Rascals, and even gets Goatee's attention. Ambo and Hawkins arrive first. Seeing Peter and Tinker Bell, they shout, "BANGARANG, BANGARANG!"

The boys catch up and run toward Peter and Tinker Bell. There is so much excitement that Goatee kicks and jumps around on all fours. Tinker Bell arrogantly hovers above Peter's head, folds her arms, lifts an eyebrow and shouts, "I told you I'd bring him back!"

Goatee accidentally kicks Brown Cow. Everyone starts laughing.

After everyone has greeted Peter, he takes a moment to return the greetings. "I have become a kid again. I sure hope I grow back up when I get home. But for now... BANGARANG!"

All of the kids and natives cheer with him.

Chapter 57

Down to Business

Peter, hands on hips, evaluates his remaining army. "Ready to go and get down to business! Tinker Bell told me what happened. Let's go get the boys back!"

"We help," says Tall Tree. "We good trackers. We find 'em."

Tootles is not too excited about dealing with pirates, especially Hook. At his age he isn't thrilled by the prospect of searching the whole island. "Too much adventure for me, so I'll stay here to keep guard over our home. I'll be here in case some slimy, sneaky pirates come sneakin' 'round."

Peter understands. "That's a good idea, Tootles. I should've thought about that myself." He winks at Tinker Bell and continues. "Someone has to stay here and keep an eye out for us, and I think you're the best man for the job. Now get me out of these clothes. Where are my old clothes?"

*　*　*　*

It is still morning as they start out. All walk single-file with Brown Cow and Tall Tree in the lead, followed by Peter and Tinker Bell, then Hawkins and Ambo. The natives are very serious and not subject to laughing or making jokes. Brown Cow looks up at Tall Tree. "This be easy trail to follow."

Tall Tree rubs his chin and looks down at Brown Cow. "Hmmmm, maybe too easy. Watch for bad sign."

The trail leads them through the forest and into the mountains, where the snow is very deep. Near the top they look down to a breathtaking view of the entire island—sparkling waterfalls, lush green jungles, clear turquoise waters flowing from waterfalls into rivers and lakes that appears to have no beginning or end. The gently floating clouds in the clear blue sky glow with the reflection of the multicolored flora below.

The natives continue to the summit, where they carefully peek over the edge. Tall Tree looks down at Brown Cow. "How we get down there? That plenty steep trail. Pirates plenty crazy."

Tinker Bell flies above them. "Pirates may be crazy, but if they can do it, so can you."

Brown Cow grunts his dismay. "Tinker Bell have wings. Me not crazy."

Tall Tree laughs as Tinker Bell slaps her forehead and mocks him. "Ugh."

Hawkins burst out in laughter and then covers her mouth in an attempt to contain herself. Ambo chuckles, "Well, we did it and we're not crazy…much."

Hawkins chuckles as well.

Chapter 58

Out on a Limb

Peter looks around and finds a huge tree limb with good-sized branches at either end. "Get on the limb. Tinker Bell and I will push."

The natives straddle the limb, holding on to the branches. Tinker Bell and Peter shove the limb down the mountain. They hang on for dear life, hollering, as they slide at breakneck speed through the snow. Hitting a bump, their rears bounce into the air as they hang on for dear life. The limb suddenly comes to an abrupt stop at the bottom of the hill, where the snow runs out. The natives fly off the limb and crash into a tree, tumbling over each other. Brown Cow lets out a long, painful "Uuuuuugh!"

Tall Tree looks up from the ground. "Me too, ugh…" Tinker Bell and Peter fly down the hill to make sure they are okay. Tinker Bell sees them covered in snow and twigs and laughs. "Didn't know you could fly, too!"

The girls find a huge piece of bark to ride down the mountain toboggan style. They push off, holding hands, and zoom down the hill. Toward the bottom they hit a bumpy patch and begin to lose control. Spinning around, they fall off the bark and flip head-over-heels into the snow. Their faces are so covered in snow they can't see anything ahead. Brown Cow dusts off snow and picks pieces of twig from his hair. Tumbling out of control, Hawkins crashes into him, knocking him down. Ambo, only seconds behind Hawkins, rams into both of them. Brown Cow, on the bottom of the pile, moans another long and painful "Uuuuuugh…"

As they untangle themselves, Hawkins finds herself face-to-face with Brown Cow. She raises her right hand and blurts out, "How now, Brown Cow."

Ambo laughs so hard tears pour down her cheeks as she rolls around on the ground holding her belly and repeats, "How now, Brown Cow."

Peter sees this. Thinking Ambo is injured, he rushes over to help her. When he realizes she is not hurt, he laughs too. "Holy cow, Brown Cow! Glad you're okay, too."

Brown Cow gets up and indignantly brushes himself off again, puffs himself up, and looks everyone up and down sternly. "Me Brown Cow, not 'holy' cow. Ugh!"

Tinker Bell watches the whole thing. She cocks her head and this time raises both eyebrows while crossing her arms. "Someone, please rescue me from this rescue team!"

* * * *

About midday they follow the trail across a clearing to where the swamp begins. Hawkins points to a large hand-painted sign that reads, THE SWAMP. "Here we go again. Let's pretend it's a food-fight and have fun in it."

Ambo grins. "Bet I can sling more mud than you can."

"Then it's on!"

Brown Cow hears the girls giggle. "Ugh! No mud! No food-fight! Now time to find Rascals!"

Tall Tree agrees, but frowns and is not happy about tramping through the mud. "The path goes this way. If girls can, we go now, get Rascals."

The natives take the lead as Tinker Bell follows from above. Peter and the girls also make their way through the swamp. They fall down often, getting dirtier and dirtier as they move slowly through the deep, deep mud. At times they are barely able to move, struggling for every forward step.

"This is the worst part of the trail," Ambo says.

Chapter 59

Into the Jungle

Peter looks up and notices vines hanging above the swamp. "Tinker Bell, how about if they hold on to a vine? We could fly everyone over the swamp."

Tinker Bell looks up. "It sure would make it easier."

"Where were you when Ambo and I came through?" Hawkins interjects.

Peter pulls out his knife. "I'll fly up and cut a strong vine, then I'll drop it down for them to hang on to."

"We'll grab the ends and tow them along," says Tinker Bell.

"Yep," says Hawkins, "that would sure make us float-ier!"

Peter cuts the vine and drops it down. Tinker Bell grabs one end; Peter takes the other. The natives look at each other, shrugging their shoulders. They grab the vine, and the girls do the same. Tinker Bell sprinkles fairy dust on them to help them get "float-ier." Peter and Tinker Bell stretch the vine tight, each securing an end. Brown Cow dangles in mid-air as he is lifted up. Tall Tree brushes the mud lightly with his feet. Brown Cow and the girls hang on behind Tall Tree but can't see beyond him.

Brown Cow's foot suddenly hits a stump protruding above the mud. "Ow, mean Ugh! Hey, Tall Tree, let me know when stump coming!"

The girls giggle. Hawkins is too short to have that problem, and Ambo is smart enough to wrap her feet up around the vine.

"How are you all doing?" Peter asks.

"We are doing just 'vine.' Ha!" Ambo replies.

Brown Cow gives a little chuckle.

After some time they reach the end of the swamp. Tinker Bell lowers her end of the vine to let the company slide off onto solid earth. Peter lets go. They all fall to the ground, tumbling over each other. The girls end up on top of the natives. Brown Cow, once again on the bottom of the pile, moans another long, painful "Uuuuuugh…"

As they untangle themselves, Hawkins finds herself face-to-face with Brown Cow—again. Again she raises her right hand and begins to say, "How now—"

Brown Cow raises his hand and interrupts her. "No 'how now,' now."

Getting up, they try to brush themselves off, but the mud has dried and encrusted on them. Tall Tree reaches down to Brown Cow and grabs a handful of dry mud off the top of his head. "This not good. Small stream ahead in jungle. We stop, all wash there."

Brown Cow looks up at Tall Tree. "I know where jungle start."

Tall Tree shakes his head. "How you know?"

Brown Cow points ahead to a hand-painted sign. "Sign say so."

*　*　*　*

Later that afternoon, Bangarangatang watches from high up in a jungle tree. He has been the sole witness to the Rascals' capture. He watches as the search team passes below in single-file. The natives have picked up the trail again, leading the search party onward. Bangarangatang observes as the girls pass below, followed by Tinker Bell, who is darting back-and-forth from the girls to the natives and back to the last person in line.

Dumbfounded, the monkey shakes his head in disbelief. It's Peter! He rubs his eyes and does a double-take to be sure he is seeing correctly. He jumps down several branches to a lower limb, chattering all the way, and finally holds his hand out to Peter, who looks up and high-fives his old friend before catching up to the group. They continue deeper and deeper into the wild as signs of evening slowly creep across the jungle floor.

*   *   *   *

The eerie shadows of dusk have begun to make the natives a little uneasy. They sense something is wrong, but can't figure out what. They whisper between themselves.

"Trail too easy," says Tall Tree. "Something wrong."

Brown Cow nods in agreement. "Maybe we should not lead anymore."

Peter approaches them to find out what is wrong. "Trail too easy," Tall Tree reiterates. "Something wrong."

"I'll take the lead."

The natives are relieved. Brown Cow takes a deep breath. "Me glad. Ugh."

Tall Tree looks down at him. "Why you always have to say, 'Ugh'?"

Brown Cow shrugs his shoulders. "Seem like thing to say!"

*   *   *   *

Peter enters a clearing, where it is very quiet. He looks across it, spots PJ's and Sneezer tied to the tree, and runs toward them. "I found them!" In his excitement he forgets to fly. He runs faster and faster toward the boys.

Tinker Bell, realizing impending danger, frantically yells out, "Fly, Peter, fly!"

But it's too late. The ground under his feet gives way, and he falls into the pit. When he realizes what is happening, he stops himself before he hits bottom, hovers in mid-air, looks up at the opening of the pit, and starts to fly up and out. Then, in a flash, a huge net drops down over him, forcing him to the bottom. The pirates, who are now looking over the edge, watch Peter struggle to get free. Bursting with laughter, they congratulate themselves and sing:

Peter Pan! Peter Pan!

We knew we could, we know'd we can!

We have captured Peter Pan!

Chapter 60

Peter in the Pit

Tinker Bell takes charge. "Hide! Hurry, hide yourselves!"

Ambo ducks into the underbrush and whispers, "Hawkins, where are you?"

The natives took refuge under some giant leaves. Hawkins stands in front of Ambo's hiding place and clenches her fists. "If I get my hands on them, I'll rip their lip!"

Ambo peeks out from the underbrush and grabs her. "Not right now, you won't! Get down here and hide with me." Hawkins drops down and crawls in with Ambo.

Peter struggles to untangle himself from the net, but the harder he tries, the more tangled he gets. If only he could reach the knife in his belt! The struggle is wearying his arms and hands. He is wrapped up like a gift for Hook. Escape is not possible now. Yet he tries not to give in. "You won't get away with this, you ugly bunch of slimy sea-rats!"

The pirates emerge from the forest to gawk and jeer at their catch. A tall pirate with a curly mustache and a long scar on his cheek points to Peter in the pit. "Argh! We put the ban on Peter Pan." A midget pirate mocks Peter with a rhyme:

This Peter Pan took Hook's hand,

But with Hook is where we stand.

We say Hook is Neverland!"

Several pirates retreat from the pit, clearing space for Hook, who is delighted at Peter trussed up in the net. "Well, well what do we have here? Something for Davy Jones?"

A short, fat pirate from behind Hook hollers out, "Argh, Cap'n! The plank! Make him walk the plank! Har, har, har!"

A pirate off to the side growls, "Dump him deep into the sea! Shark bait he'd be!"

Hand on hip, Hook gazes down at his new prisoner. "Lookin' plenty pit-i-ful in the pit, eh, Peter? Pit-is-full, all right! Full of the Pan! Argh!"

"You won't get away with this, Hook!"

"I already have, Peteeee Boy! Thought it was over, didn't you? You see, Ieeee am Neverland."

"You may have the upper hand—or should I say the upper hook—right now, but not for long. Your end is coming, and I will see to it!"

Hook is silent. All the pirates silently wait for Hook's response. Peter himself is impatient for Hook's next words. Then Hook breaks the silence with a loud laugh. "Somehow I don't think so! Children will read, 'This was the end of Peter Pan.' Argh!"

"Hook, Hook, Hooray!" the pirates cheer. "The Hook is back!"

"And maybe I'll cut off your other hand!"

The pirates boo and hiss at Peter's most outrageous statement. Above the din a pirate's voice is heard, "Give 'im yer blade, Cap'n!"

The still-tangled Peter is raised from the pit. An impatient, very agitated Hook rubs his hook. "Not this day. Take him to the ship! Away with him!"

Sparky and Jenks stand in back, watching Peter trussed up and hung from a large limb, like a pig on a spit. "I don't like this, Sparky," Jenks whispers. "I don't like it at all."

Sparky shakes his head. "We're doomed."

The pirates disappear into the jungle with their captive. Tinker Bell and the girls watch in horror as he is carried away. Brown Cow shakes his head. "This not good."

Tinker Bell, frightened, frantically darts all around. "This is awful! We must do something right away! We have to help Peter!"

Tall Tree makes a decision: "We go back to Rascals home. Make plan, help Peter."

"That good thinking, Tall Tree," says Ambo. "Home closer to dock." Then she mumbles to herself, "Why me talk this way?"

Brown Cow nods. "Ugh…"

"Always 'ugh'!" Tall Tree says, agitated. "Why you can't say anything but 'ugh'?"

Brown Cow just shrugs his shoulders. "Ugh?"

Tall Tree rolls his eyes. "Maybe only thing to say to that is…ugh! We go now."

Tinker Bell and the girls follow as Tall Tree and Brown Cow lead them back to the Neverland Rascals' home.

Chapter 61

Jenks' Key to Life

Puff and the Rascals sit on the floor of the ship's brig in low spirits, hungry, wondering what their end will be. Their only hope is for Tinker Bell, the girls and the natives to figure out a way to help them.

Meanwhile, Jenks and another pirate appear with loaves of bread and a bucket of water. The other pirate, with a huge nose, sets the bucket on the floor and runs a metal cup across the bars, making a loud racket. "Get up, you worthless lot of mangy mutts! Supper's here!"

The Rascals, seeing the big nose, snicker and laugh. The pirate's face turns red. "Think me nose is funny, do ya? Me nose knows what nobody else knows. And this nose knows what's to happen to you! Argh!"

Whippy is still laughing. "Anyone 'knows' what the nose just said?"

Jenks feigns anger. "Better settle down in there! I got bread here, and it's 'breader' than nothing!" He passes the loaves through to the Rascals. "Here's yer water cup, too! You'll all drink from it! And there's yer bucket of water, and pay no mind to those strange floaties in 'er."

With a bit of flair Jenks motions to the other pirate that it's time to leave, and then points at Puff, who is about to take a big bite out of the loaf passed to him. "That there bread is yer key to life, boy."

The two pirates disappear. PJ's ferociously gobbles down the bread, "Wish

I could magically change this bread, but it's…'breader' than nothin'."

Puff chomps into his loaf and yelps, "What the…" Clearly he's bitten into something very hard. He pokes around in the bread, only to discover a large piece of metal. Looking around to be sure no pirates can see, he pulls the object out of the loaf.

It's a key!

He recalls what Jenks said: "That there bread is yer key to life." The Rascals gather around Puff silently. "This will open the cell door," he declares. Then he uses hand signals and body language to indicate their escape plan. He opens the door, and they all follow him out. He tries the key in the next cell, but it doesn't work. So he whispers, "We'll come back as soon as possible and somehow get you out."

Chapter 62

Breaking Out to Break In

It is night. In the moonlight the pirates are here and there on deck, and some are out on the dock. None suspect any trouble, and they pay no attention to what little movement is on deck. Puff and the boys manage to stay low, ducking behind the rigging and barrels as they finally reach the gangplank. They look around and see only a few pirates on the dock engrossed in conversation. No one on deck has noticed them.

Then, at the opportune moment, they hardly make a sound as they sneak down the gangplank to the dock. Cautiously, they pass the conversing pirates and disappear into the streets. One pirate catches a glimpse of them running and points down the street. "I'll be flogged if them weren't some of those brats gettin' away!"

One rather chubby pirate who is gnawing on a turkey leg shouts, "Someone find Hook and tell him!"

A very tall, skinny pirate answers, "No way! You go tell Hook."

Finally, that red-bearded pirate named The Red says, "Both of you zip yer flappin' lips! I'll go. I'll tell Hook you let 'em go. Argh!"

* * * *

After a long trek in the jungle, The Red reaches the edge of Hook's encampment, where merriment is in the air. Pirates dance about the campfire while others drink grog and clink their mugs. As The Red gets closer in, he notices Peter trussed up on a large limb like a spitted pig. He sees Hook, who appears very happy. The Red has second thoughts about breaking bad news to Hook when he is in such a good mood.

Hook lifts his mug when he sees The Red approach. "Well, if it isn't The Red come to join in the celebration! Come on, lad, have a mug of grog."

Now The Red is really afraid to tell Hook, but he forges ahead anyway: "Cap'n, some of those Rascals got away! Some others weren't watchin'."

Hook pauses, then laughs. "Let them run away! We've got Peter Pan."

Relieved that Hook isn't angry, The Red raises his fist. "The Hook is back!"

Hook hands The Red a mug full to the brim with grog as the other pirates chant, "Hook, Hook, Hook is back!" Hook twists his hook in time with the chant.

*   *   *   *

The next morning, the pirates start back to the village. Bangarangatang again runs up a tree as Hook's entourage passes by. Sparky and Jenks bring up the rear, Sparky ahead of Jenks. The monkey sees Sparky and climbs down to make faces, laugh and throw sticks at him. Then he mocks Sparky with flips and jumps above him, bends over and wiggles his rear end at him. Jenks chuckles to himself at this hilarity.

"Monkey doomed," Sparky says slowly in a monotone. He looks back at Jenks, grabs a stick with unbelievable speed, and flings it with spot-on accuracy into Bangarangatang's rear end. The monkey lets out a blood-curdling scream as he scurries up the tree with the stick lodged between his buttocks. Sparky looks back at Jenks, murmurs a low grunt, and keeps on going. Jenks raises his unibrow, amazed at Sparky's speed and accuracy.

Chapter 63

Gorilla War

The setting sun shines through the leaves and branches of the trees surrounding the Rascals' home. Crane, Puff and the other escapees have rested and are now eating an impromptu meal imagined by Tootles.

As they finish, Tinker Bell, the girls and the two natives arrive. Tinker Bell is surprised to see them. "How did you boys get away? We thought we'd never see you again."

The boys began to answer, but Ambo interrupts them: "Can't we talk about that later? Hook has Peter! We've got to rescue him!"

Puff is startled by the news. "Hook has Peter?" He puts his hand on his sword. "This is war! We have to plan a rescue!"

Incredulous that Peter has actually been captured, everyone agrees to Puff's proposal except Tootles, who hangs his head in discouragement and shrugs his shoulders. "There are not enough of us for a war!"

"April War!" Hawkins blurts.

"Not April War!" says Ambo. "Gorilla War!"

Tinker Bell lands on the table. "Yeah, Gorilla War! But what's April War?"

Ambo chuckles. "We'll explain that one later."

Puff raises his fist. "Hook has Peter, but not for long."

Crane raises his fist and adds, "Gorilla War will right the wrong!"

Getting the drift, all raise their fists high in the air, shouting, "BANGARANG!" Puff jumps up on the table, both arms raised. "Let's get ready for war! BANGARANG!"

* * * *

Hiding behind some barrels on the dock the next morning, a small band of Rascal boys dressed as pirates prepare to take action. Puff and Crane left the group to sneak aboard Hook's ship. No guards are on the dock, and the boys easily got to the ship, as it is docked now. Several pirates are sleeping on the deck, around the open hatch. Puff and Crane lean over it and listen. Soon they hear a couple of pirates talking below: "What a great day for Hook! Pan is hooked! Argh!"

Puff puts his fingers to his lips and motions for Crane to move forward and listen with him.

"Har! He'll never escape. He's at the bottom of the ship."

"Soon to be at the bottom of the sea, matey."

The boys look at each other, nod, and retreat to the dock. Safely returning, they report to the Rascals and Tinker Bell, who is hardly able to contain herself. "Did you see Peter? Could you find him?"

"No, but we heard a couple of pirates talking," says Puff.

Tinker Bell is still very excited. "Well, what did they say? What did they say?"

"Give me a chance! They've got him down in the bottom of the ship, and it sounds like Hook's going to make Peter—ah—"

Crane interjects. "Sounds like Hook's going to make Peter walk the plank!"

Tall Tree sits straight up. "Walk plank? Oh, no! Peter become plankton!"

Brown Cow says, "Ugh—"

Tall Tree swats Brown Cow on the back of the head. Brown Cow takes a deep breath and looks up and down his tall friend with a frown.

Crane offers a rescue plan. "Maybe we can cut a hole in the bottom of the ship and get Peter out that way."

Tinker Bell shakes her head. "No, that won't work. You'll sink the ship, the boys and Peter with it!"

Puff rubs his chin as he starts to think out loud: "There has to be a way before Hook carries out his plan."

Crane mimics Puff's gesture. "But how…how?"

Brown Cow raises his hand. "How!"

In frustration, Tall Tree reaches over and slaps Brown Cow across the back of the head once again. "Now not the time to say 'how'!"

Brown Cow takes a deep breath, puffs out his chest, and looks up and down Tall Tree with a frown.

Tootles is getting antsy. "Well, you boys know the ship's layout. What do you think we can do?"

Crane thinks out loud again: "Hook hates Peter so much that maybe he'll make a mistake. That kind of hate blinds people."

"Yes, that's true, but we can't wait for a 'maybe.' We have to act now!"

Tain speaks up. "I know what we can do to rescue Peter. Listen up, here's my plan." They all huddle close together as Tain whispers his scheme. At one point Tinker Bell's voice is heard above the others: "Wisdom comes from being around awhile."

"Ha! At my age, I must have plenty of wisdom. People always tell me I'm full of it," jokes Tootles.

Tinker Bell and Crane chuckle, but when all is said, all agree with

Tain's plan. Then, careful to keep things quiet, they whisper in unison, "BANGARANG!"

Chapter 64

On-board Celebration

Late that afternoon, a party is in full swing on Hook's ship. Pirates are eating and drinking, dancing and singing, celebrating Peter's capture. Some are fooling around and dance out onto the plank. A rather large, boisterous pirate loses his balance, and over he goes, causing a huge splash. Many pirates burst into laughter.

From the ship's upper deck, Smee sports a great big smile and says to Hook, "Aye Cap'n, what a grand party in your honor!"

Twirling his hook, Hook responds, "Yes, my honor, indeed."

"Is it time to do the Pan in?"

"Yesss, soon, very soon. But first I feel a speech coming on."

Smee leans over the rail to flag the crew's attention by raising his hands. "Hold on, mates! I feel an announcement coming! Listen up, lads! Master, Commander and Wonder of the Seven Seas, Neverland himself, Cap'n Hook, has somethin' he wants to say and will have a word with ya!"

Taking bows as he approaches the rail, Hook looks over the pirates on the lower deck and over at those on the dock. His evil smile curls on his lips as he whispers to Smee, "Quite right, all true."

The pirates are still noisy, so Smee again raises his hands to hush them and yells out, "Listen up, ya parasitic, bottom-feeding sea-slime! Lift yer ale mugs to the Cap'n!"

Laughter mocking Smee rises from the crew. Hook bumps him aside, raises his arms, and motions for the men to settle down. Slowly, the noise diminishes, and ale mugs are raised to honor Hook. "Speech, speech!" several pirates holler.

Hook, in the pretense of grandeur, arrogantly responds, "Thank you friends, thank you. I'm going to make a speech in honor of this occasion. I, The Hook, Master, Commander, Wonder of the Seven Seas and Neverland itself, am the only one who could ever have captured Peter Pan!"

Smee whispers to Hook, "A bit much, don't you think, Cap'n?"

Hook turns to glare at his mate. "I think not."

Feeling the sting of a threat, Smee backs away. "Okay, Cap'n, okay."

As Hook turns back to his crew, the pirates chant, "Hook, Hook, Hook is back! The Hook is back! Hook, Hook, Hook is back!" over and over again as they dance and lift ale mugs to Hook, who twists his hook for several long seconds to the music, reveling in the recognition. Suddenly raising his arms, he quiets them.

"Everyone thought my end in sight when the crocodile swallowed me alive. But I am, and will always be, Neverland. The croc dried on the dock, and Peter will go to Davy Jones' locker. There is none like me! I am the Hook! I am Neverland!"

Chapter 65

A Flickering Light of Hope

At the bottom of the ship, a musty stench permeates the air. Peter is locked up in a dark, dingy cell, still net-bound. The cell is wet. Rats run all around.

A flicker of light from a small candle dances on the cell wall, getting closer and closer. Peter gets a sudden fright as Jenks appears, holding a lit candle just under his chin, which makes his face look as if it grew even more gruesome. Nervously standing at the cell door, Jenks shyly smiles and places a key in the cell door. Peter peers through the net to see Jenks unlocking the cell.

"Time to fight, time to crow, time to fly, time to go!" Jenks whispers.

Peter doesn't know what to think. "What's going on here? What are you doing?"

"It's all wrong." Looking all around, Jenks enters the cell, his feet slapping the wet floor. He pulls out his very sharp potato-peeling knife as he approaches Peter's net. "It's just wrong, I say, just wrong!"

Peter nervously keeps his eye on the knife. "Are you going to do me in right here?"

By now Jenks' knife blade is now on Peter's neck, but Jenks is silent. Both look each other in the eye for a moment. Peter closes his eyes as he waits for the worst. Jenks cuts Peter out of the net.

Opening his eyes, Peter is astonished. "Why are you doing this? Aren't you one of Hook's pirates?"

Jenks then severs the rope from Peter's wrists. Peter rubs them as he stands and stretches sideways and down to get his circulation going, still unsure why this pirate is freeing him. "Who are you?"

Jenks shushes him with his finger on Peter's nose, missing his lips. "Don't tell nobody, but I'm Jenks, and I'm tired of Hook's abuse. It's my turn to take control."

Peter looks cross-eyed at Jenks' finger and then gently moves it away. "Your turn? I don't understand."

Jenks leans closer to Peter. "Always do what's right. Even when they treat you wrong."

Peter puts his hand on Jenks' shoulder. "You have a good heart, friend, and I am very appreciative. How can I ever thank you?"

Chapter 66

Time to Fight, Crow, Fly, and Go

Peter, hands on hips, looks across to the cell where the remaining Rascals are held. "Time to fly, and time to go." He cautiously looks around as he crosses with Jenks to the other side. Jenks, fumbling with the keys on a huge ring, slips in a small puddle of mucky water, sending the keys up in the air. In an attempt to catch them as they fall, he accidentally bumps into Peter and pushes him back a few steps. The keys land soundly on the grid with a loud clank. Peter cautiously looks around to make sure the pirates above didn't hear the noise. Then he nods the all-clear.

Jenks tiptoes to the cell. "I'll open the door and free the lads," he whispers.

Peter points to a pile of weapons against the wall by a large wooden door and motions for Jenks to stay put as he whispers, "Where does this door go?"

Jenks nods his head, standing there a moment with a goofy satisfied look on his face. "Out! It goes out!" Realizing he has shouted, he puts his fingers to his own lips, shushing himself. Peter nods and motions for Jenks to follow him.

Turning to the kids in the now-unlocked cell, Jenks gestures for them to stay inside and wait for the signal from Peter. Jenks clumsily avoids another puddle of mucky water and trips over his own foot, landing on the pile of weapons. Once again, he realizes he has created a clamor. He puts his fingers to his face, missing his lips and landing on his nose. Looking cross-eyed at his own fingers, he again shushes himself.

*　*　*　*

Meanwhile, up on the captain's deck, Hook is about to give another speech. Smee stretches out his arms to quiet the pirate crew. The dancing and singing stop as the pirates gather round to hear Hook, who says loudly and proudly, "The time has come! All that has been and is supposed to be has come to this moment! This is my war and victory, now for us all to see!"

"Victory for all!" the pirates chant. "Victory for all!"

Hook resumes his speech. "The moment of my glorious victory. I am this day doing away with Peter Pan, once and for all." A snarly smile appears on his face as he raises his hook to the sky in a gesture of victory. "Har! This day is mine, all mine! I am Neverland!"

Smee again raises his hands, this time to get a great pirate cheer for Hook. A pirate voice from the main deck shouts: "Peter Pan cut off his hand! Now no one will give Peter a hand! Hook is back!"

"Hook is back! Hook is back!"

Sparky, who is on the deck below Hook, mutters under his breath, "We're all doomed. Uuuuugh."

A pirate near Sparky asks him, "What's the mudder with you?"

Sparky is confused. "What's my mudder got to do with it?"

The other pirate walks away, now utterly confused himself.

"Your mudder? Uuuuugh!"

Chapter 67

Hook Don't Know What's Below

Hook has both arms in the air. "Now is the time! Bring him up! Today I will cut off his life!"

Two pirates walk over to open the door, but just as one reaches over to grab the handle, Peter, who was waiting for the right moment, bursts through the door and knocks both of them down. He stands in front of the pirate crew, both hands on his hips, as he looks around, summing up his situation. Before anyone can lay hands on him, he is off and away. Passing Hook's face, he reaches out ever so close and knocks the hat right off Hook's head. Smee scurries to pick up the hat. He gets it back up on Hook's head, but it is crooked and sideways.

Hook, looking angry and anguished, uses his hook to whack it into place.

"We're doomed now," Sparky mutters again. "Uuurrr."

"Not again!" says the other pirate. "I don't even want to know!"

Chaos and pandemonium reign on the main deck as the pirates realize Peter is free and laughing from midway up the mast. They go after him, but he flies higher to the top. Hook watches in total disbelief. Peter laughs at the chaos below from his high perch.

Hook points skyward from his balcony. "He is there! Get him, get him!"

Some of the pirates start to climb the mast while others pull out their guns and shoot. They all miss as Peter moves and dodges. Another pirate aims the cannon at Peter and fires. He misses Peter but hits the mast in the middle. More bedlam erupts as the mast falls past Hook to the main deck. The pirates scramble for safety from the falling timber.

"No! No! This can't happen!" Hook shouts.

As the pirate crew searches the sky for Peter, the door on deck suddenly bursts open again. The Rascals, armed with various weapons, come out fighting. Jenks, staying low, sneaks out behind them without anyone seeing him. Hook and Smee watch the melee below. The Rascals push back the pirates enough to escape to the dock and join the others as they come out from hiding. Peter lands on the railing several feet away, just out of Hook's immediate reach.

Hook drives his hook into the railing and shouts, "Someone is responsible for this, and I will find you! I hate—I hate—I hate Peter Pan!" Realizing Peter has been standing on the railing, he draws his sword. "You! It's you, Pan! You're the one responsible."

Peter draws his own sword. "One more time, James Hook. This time will end it."

The pirate crew and the Rascals slowly realize this battle is not theirs, but between Hook and Peter. They stop fighting and follow the two as the skirmish ensues.

Chapter 68

Peter Learns a New Lesson

Peter and Hook battle all over the ship, from the captain's deck to the main deck, down the ramp and onto the dock, out onto the street, and back onto the dock. It is a long, hard fight. The pirate crew loudly cheers for Hook.

At one tense moment, Hook manages to whack Peter's sword up and into the air. As Hook tries to strike again, Peter flies up and grabs his sword out of midair. The Rascals cheer and encourage Peter with shouts of "BANGARANG!"

At one point Peter is standing on the edge of a wooden plank extending out beyond the others. Hook stands at the other end. Peter jumps on the end of the plank, and it flips the other end up, hits Hook's hand with the sword, and knocks it into his face. The Rascals all laugh as Hook hollers, "Argh, bad form!" and rubs his chin.

The battle continues on the dock, where Bangarangatang is jumping and flipping over the excitement. A crowd of more pirates and villagers gathers.

Peter gets an upper hand and backs Hook into the dried-up crocodile from which he escaped. He is now sitting on the ground, pinned against the croc, with the tip of Peter's sword at his throat. "You, your hook and your sword are done forever!" Peter shouts. For a moment Hook has terror in his eyes.

Just as Peter is ready to pierce Hook's throat and end it, Jenks steps in, puts his hand on Peter's shoulder, and says softly, "Peter, forgive Hook, or you'll never be free."

"Forgive Hook? Never! He dies now, and it's over!"

"No, Peter, it's not only about Hook. You'll never be free until you forgive."

Hook, with his evil smile, now starts to mock Peter, thinking he will do just the opposite of what he says. "Kill me, Peter. Don't listen to him. He's wrong. Death is the only adventure left for me."

"It's not for Hook alone," Jenks says to Peter. "It's for your freedom."

Peter's face is twisted with hatred toward Hook. He hesitates, but again it seems he will run Hook through anyway as Jenks' words swirl in his head. He stops again and shakes his head. His look of hardness and hatred slowly softens as he begins to understand Jenks' wisdom.

Hook, knowing the truth of Jenks' words, tries to mock, provoke and confuse Peter again. "Death is the only great adventure left for me. Strike true, Peter."

Peter looks back at Jenks, who nods and gestures for Peter to back off. Peter steps back a little. "You're right, Jenks. Hook's death won't free me."

Jenks nods and winks. Peter feels his anger fade. "Forgiving Hook will. I can see that now. I would be like Hook. Even when I thought Hook was dead, the hatred was ruining my life."

Hook points at him. "Peter, we must continue the war. Give me my sword. The war must be finished."

"You're wrong, Hook. I understand now. Forgiveness is freedom. We all need to learn this."

"Peter, I can't believe, after everything I've done to you and the Rascals, that you would forgive me."

"I must forgive you, Hook. To be free, I must!"

Hook coquettishly tips his head. "Can you really forgive me—The Hook?"

Suddenly, Peter steps forward and lays his sword at Hook's throat again. Jenks, astonished, backs up out of the way and goes to stand next to Sparky.

"Hook," Peter asserts, "you must promise to change your ways if you want to live."

"I need to think on this a moment."

"You'd better think quick."

Hook, with his protruding toothy smile, taps his nose, rubs his chin, looks up at Peter, and then stands up. "What would Neverland do without me? So our war is over? Considering your good form, Peter...I agree."

Peter nods, sheathes his sword, turns to join the Rascals, and explains to them, "With hatred in your heart, you will never be free, even if you win."

Chapter 69

Pops is Back

Puff knew Peter would eventually have to depart. "You're going to leave us now, aren't you?"

Peter smiles. "Yes, but I'll be back. I'll never forget you. Always remember this lesson we learned today."

"We'll never forget you either, Peter," Tain sadly says.

In unison, they all yell together, "BANGARANG!"

Tinker Bell flies down to Peter, who looks at her remorsefully. "I've got to get back to my family, Tinker Bell. You and the boys are family, too. Take good care of them."

She is sad. "You will come back again, Peter, won't you?"

"Yes, Tinker Bell. As I told the Rascals, I will never forget, and some day soon I will be back."

"I know you will, and when you do…BANGARANG!"

"I'll have to get my old clothes. These won't work well if I change back." Tinker Bell and the Rascals just snicker. He heads back to the treehouse. In a short while they all see Peter leaving.

As he disappears through the rainbow flash, he is transformed back to his adult self. Looking at his hands, he says to himself, "Amazing!"

* * * *

The sun peeks over the horizon as the nighttime stars disappear one by one. A crisp, clean chill is in the air. Another fine morning dawns in England as Peter hovers over Wendy's house, taking in the beauty. He quietly descends and lands onto the balcony outside his children's room. He peeks through the panes of the French window and clearly sees them in their beds, warm and cozy. Feeling peaceful, Peter can still hear Jenks' words: "Forgive Hook, or you'll never be free." The same peaceful sleep will now be his, too, with the issue of Hook settled once and for all.

He taps on the glass. The children begin to stir. Their eyes are still sleepy as they rub the sand from them, and they have what Peter calls "morning face." He taps again. A face appears, staring out at Peter through the window.

"Dad?" Clint presses his face to the glass and rubs his eyes once more. "It's Dad!"

Peter grins from ear to ear, nods his head, and points to the door latch. Clint excitedly shouts to Amber, "Dad's back!"

Amber is just awakening. "What? Pops is back? Pops is back!" They happily hop around and call out, "Dad is back!" Clint runs to get Mom and Wendy, forgetting to unlock the French window. Amber, realizing Pops is still outside in the cold, runs to let him in. Trish hears the commotion and runs into the room as Peter enters. The children and Trish all hug Peter and each other, jumping around with excitement.

"Peter, I'm so glad you're back!" whispers Trish. "I was so worried!"

Peter hugs and kisses his wife in return and whispers, "I'm glad to be back, too, but you shouldn't have worried so."

Wendy enters the room and joins in the embracing and excitement. "Welcome home, Peter! Let's all go downstairs, and I'll fix breakfast. You are hungry, aren't you?"

Chapter 70

"You Have Ties to Neverland"

The children and Wendy lead the way downstairs toward the kitchen. Trish and Peter follow, arm in arm. Trish stops on the landing and snuggles into Peter's chest. "Did everything go the way you expected?"

"No, as a matter of fact, not at all like I expected."

Startled by his response, Trish presses him for an explanation. "I don't understand. What do you mean by that?"

Peter can understand her confusion. "You see, there was this old snaggle-toothed pirate that actually had a good heart and meant well. His words turned my world of anger upside-down. He made me realize that the onus was on me."

Confused, Trish and Wendy shake their heads at each other. Peter tries to clarify. "This pirate named Jenks, a really common character with no formal education, got my undivided attention with one singular word of wisdom: 'Forgive.'"

Both women stare at Peter in awe. Wendy gently ventures, "Forgive what?"

"Jenks' very own words to me were, 'Peter, it's not only about Hook. You'll never be free until you forgive Hook.'"

Trish and Wendy are amazed at the simplicity of the statement: Forgiveness is Freedom! Wendy looks at Peter with her head cocked to one side. "Happy thoughts, Peter?"

He smiles. "Yes, Wendy, all happy thoughts. Happy thoughts in my happy place."

"And a happy face, too!" Wendy ads.

"A free and happy face, too." Peter sighs.

Peter, Wendy and Trish stand arm in arm, looking up at the stained-glass window for a moment. "So, Peter, are the adventures over this time?" Wendy inquires.

Peter gazes up at the window, as if in deep thought about the question. Everyone awaits his answer, which he finally offers matter-of-factly: "Don't know about that, Wendy. Our family is an adventure."

Trish smiles and raises her eyebrows. "Life with Peter Pan is an adventure in itself."

The trio enter the kitchen. Clint is helping Amber wash the dishes. "Wow, that's great!" says Peter. "Doing dishes without being told, and we haven't even eaten yet!"

Clint nods, smiling. Amber says, "Well, we don't always have to be told. Sometimes we just do it."

With serious curiosity Clint asks, "Will you ever go back to Neverland, Dad?"

Peter rubs his son's head. "I suppose I will, when the time is right."

"Oh, no, Peter, not again," says Trish, worried.

"Trish, I would like to go back, when I can."

Amber follows up on Peter's good mood. "Dad, can we go too, please?"

Peter puts his hand on his daughter's shoulder, "Yes, there is a very strong possibility that you could go."

Trish frowns. "No way."

Peter grins. "Trish, you could go too."

Excited, the children dance around their mother. Then they each take one of her hands and lead her back to the stairs, pointing to the stained-glass window. Peter and Wendy follow. Trish quietly stares at the window, her hand on her chest. A small smile crosses her face as she turns to her husband. "Me? Really! You think I could go?"

Peter looks at Wendy and nods with a mischievous smile on his face. Wendy, reading Peter's mind, wiggles her finger at him. "Oh, no you don't! Not me! I'm too old!"

Peter laughs. "You certainly know you're never too old in Neverland."

Trish happily agrees. "You're never too old!"

Peter is enjoying the excitement. "Come on, Grammy Wendy! One more great Neverland adventure together, all of us. Remember your song, 'Antique Little Girl'?"

Wendy shrugs her shoulders as she looks at the kids. "Well, I don't know." She looks back up at the window "But, just maybe."

After a few moments of contemplative silence and looking at each other, the whole family begins to laugh. The thought of another adventure that includes everyone is delightful. The children are so excited they hug each other.

Then Clint, realizing he actually hugged his sister, exclaims, "Ugh!" as he backs away and puts her at arm's length.

Amber just laughs at him and says, "It's not 'Ugh,' it is 'How... Wait... Where did I get that from?' "

Peter looks at both of them. "Neverland... Because of me, apparently you have ties to Neverland as well. I'll explain someday, but, you know, you both have similar looks, like two of the Rascals. Mmmm, naw, couldn't be."

"What, dad, what?" Amber's curiosity is piqued.

"Well, I had a brother years ago that I never knew. He passed away but had two children about your age. I guess they lost track of them."

Amber puts her hand on her heart. "I'd love to meet them. What are their names?"

Peter puts his hand on Amber's shoulder. "Ambo and Tain, but you will someday meet all of the Rascals."

Amber and Clint look at each other and smile. Clint speaks up. "We could be related to some Rascals? Good form, dad."

"Now the odds of you being related are almost impossible." Peter turns away but puts his hand on his chin. "Mmm, very interesting."

Chapter 71

A Seemingly Unrepentant Hook

The pirates are back on the ship, and all have settled down. Hook and Smee are standing on the deck. Hook has been contemplating what happened with Peter and almost feels respect for him. He still can't quite grasp how Peter could just forgive him, and it makes him think. This way of thinking is completely foreign to him. With his back to the pirates he slowly tilts his head upward, lifts his sword to his hat so the pirates won't notice, and salutes a farewell to Peter.

Glancing back at the pirates, he notices some are watching him. He knows he needs their respect, and it jolts him, and in an instant his demeanor changes as he raises his hook toward the sky. Pure evil crosses Hook's face, seemingly forgetting all of the thoughts of respect that had just crossed his mind. Sheathing his sword, he stares up at the golden rays of the rising sun reflecting off his hook.

His voice breaks the silence like a lion's roar echoing through the Village: "I hate and will always hate Peter Pan!"

Chapter 72

Peace in Neverland

As the sorrows of Peter's departure subside, the Rascals start to settle down in Neverland. Everyone is tired and ready for some rest—almost.

Tain wants peace and quiet, so he goes down to the lake, where he spent many happy hours swimming, playing and laughing. He sits atop some rocks in front of the waterfall, watching it cascade into the lake. He loves the thunder of the water crashing, creating rainbows in its misty spray. The waterfall lightly sprays on his face. The beautiful turquoise-blue lake invites him to jump in and feel the cool, clear water. In one fluid motion he is up and in, swimming around. Floating on his back, he enjoys the peace and serenity of the moment. Looking up at the clouds, he watches as they form different images in the sky.

Tain is finally at complete peace. His eyes are closed, and his imagination flows as freely as the water. He thinks of what it might have been like had the orphanage not closed. It would have been a bleak, frightening future had Tinker Bell not appeared and brought them to Neverland. He feels forever thankful and blessed to be the chosen from all of the children in the world. He will never know why or how. This is a real fairy tale touching their lives.

Without any warning, a loud, obnoxious clamor, sounding like several screaming banshees, smashes through Tain's serenity. Startled, he flails his arms, forgetting he is in the water, and begins to sink. His mouth fills with water. Realizing the source of such a commotion, he spews water from his mouth like a whale spouting from his blowhole. Several of the boys run toward the lake, peeling off their clothing as they go. Tain watches them jump in, yelling, "BANGARANG!" Goatee is with them, running back-and-forth on the shoreline, wanting to join in the fun but not liking the water. Once in the water, the boys yell and splash each other. Tain watches the melée as if in a slow-motion trance, but snaps out of it by yelling, "Stop!"

In a moment they all stop and stare at Tain. His hands are up in the air. "Mellow out! I was enjoying the peace."

The boys look at each other and then back at Tain, pausing with one more look around. Pinner hollers, "BANGARANG!" The splashing and yelling resume.

Tain begins to swim toward shore. He shakes his head in disgust as he gets out of the water. "I gotta get some privacy." He heads for the path and looks back at the commotion. "I need some peace and quiet time to think and give thanks."

Chapter 73

A Coated Tain

Down the path, ahead of Tain, about halfway between the treehouse and the lake, Aky and Sneezer are hiding in a tree, waiting for a victim to pass under them. A bucket filled with a mixture of water and flour also waits silently.

"Now be quiet, and no sneezing," Aky warns Sneezer.

Sneezer holds his finger against his upper lip. "Okie-dokie."

Aky spots Tain heading their way. "No, it's not Okydoky, its Tain."

Sneezer raises his hands. "No, I meant okay."

The boys watch Tain as he approaches. Their timing is impeccable: just as he walks underneath, the bucket of muck pours over him like a waterfall, covering him head-to-toe. Startled, he jumps, but too late. The boys laugh so hard Sneezer falls out of the tree. It is quite a sight, seeing Sneezer try to untangle himself from the bushes in his not-so-great landing area. Tain himself laughs out loud, and soon all of the boys are laughing so hard they can hardly breathe. As Tain rolls on the ground, he gets covered with leaves and twigs sticking to his flour-and-water mixture.

Catching his breath, he stands up. He looks like a scarecrow. All his serious thoughts have disappeared. He reminds himself, Nothing is worth being so worried and stressed about. Relaxed once again, he folds his hands under his head to make a pillow, lies down, looks up, and sees rays of sunshine filter through the leafy branches. Right back to peace and serenity. Ahhh, nothing like the sound of the breeze rustling through the trees.

Once again, however, chaos resounds. Sneezer sneezes, and out of nowhere, Goatee charges, horns down, heading for Sneezer right in front of Tain's feet. Sneezer is off like a bullet, running as fast as he can, with Goatee close behind as they fly down the path and disappear. Aky just shakes his head and laughs out loud. "Psycho goat!"

Tain realizes that what he just saw is relaxing, too. "Peace doesn't always have to be quiet." He chuckles and once again rests his head on his hands.

Chapter 74

"Will the Boat Float?"

Back at the lake, Big C holds his finger in the air. "I have an idea. Let's build a boat and float down the river."

"Good idea!" agrees Whippy. "Let's get started!"

The others agree. They all swim to the shore. While they dress, Whippy puts his finger in the air, mocking Big C. "Let's get back to the treehouse, get the tools, and get started."

"Very funny," Big C gruffly responds.

*   *   *   *

Back at the treehouse, the Rascals gather up tools while Whippy sketches what the boat should look like. Big C contemplates the sketch and shakes his head. Whippy glares at Big C, knowing exactly what is coming next—the finger in the air. Noticing Whippy's smirk, Big C starts to do just that but quickly changes direction and points to the drawing instead. "Not much of a drawing. Let me help."

Ambo stands off to the side, watching this whole interaction. Mildly annoyed, she sarcastically throws her hands in the air. "Wow, can we get on with this?"

Finally, Big C sits down and begins to improve on Whippy's sketch. Everyone waits patiently. After several minutes of silence and sketching, Big C calls everyone over. "Here, check this out."

They all begin to gather around. Whippy picks up the paper. "Not bad. Your sketching looks pretty good."

Big C, with his flair toward self-importance, leans toward Whippy and points his finger at the paper. "My sketches are not 'sketching.' My sketches are drawings."

At that moment his finger lunges toward the paper, poking a hole in it. Whippy yanks the paper away, shakes his head and shows everyone the drawing. "We won't put the hole in the boat Big C just added."

Everyone agrees that the sketch finally looks good, so the Rascals begin preparations for building their new boat. Whippy designates who gets what. "Kilowatts, you get some rope and nails. Big C, you get some planks. Crane, you get a blanket and some barrels. Okay, everybody meet at the lake, and we'll get started."

Everyone works diligently until the boat is finished later that afternoon. All stand back to eye their creation. "Pretty good, if I say so myself," says Whippy, arms crossed.

Big C, standing at the water's edge, puts his foot up on the side of the boat. "My drawing." His foot slips, he falls to his knees in the water, and all laugh.

The boat, a big rectangle measuring about twelve feet long and eight feet wide, has eight small wooden barrels for seats and oars cut from planks. The keel is a tree limb, and six wooden barrels are attached to the bottom of the boat for floats. The mast is a tall, crooked limb. At mid-section, another shorter limb is cross-tied to the mast, about two feet from the top. A large piece of white cloth is tied to the limb and rolled up. When unrolled about six feet, it is a sail, beautifully hand-painted in an array of brightly colored rainbows by

Ambo and Hawkins.

All rush to get into the boat. "Hold on now!" cautions Whippy. "The boat will only hold maybe eight of us. Let's draw straws to see who gets the first ride with me. Shortest straws go first."

Okydoky points at Whippy. "Ha, y'all, Whippy is now da Straw Boss?"

Whippy ignores him as the others laugh. He grabs some reeds from the water's edge and breaks them into five even pieces; the sixth is longer than the rest. Each boy picks a reed from Whippy's hand. Kilowatts, Crane, PJ's, Big C, and Okydoky get the shortest reeds. Puff, holding the last and longest reed, realizes the count is wrong, "Hey, wait a minute! We only have seven of us here, and eight can go, so we can all go."

Whippy is embarrassed. "I knew it all along."

They all just groan and enter the boat. Everyone goes to the same side, which tips the boat way over. "Spread out, you dummies!" Whippy yells. Settling in and sitting down, six of this motley green crew of shipmates grab oars, and Whippy takes the keel. The boat feels right, and this crew is anxious to shove off, unaware that things can change at a moment's notice once they are on the water.

Chapter 75

Rowing the River

"Shove off, mates!" Whippy snaps, sounding like a pirate. The water, however, is too shallow, and the boat is sitting in the sand. Crane and Puff dig their oars into the sand, hoping to move the vessel, but no luck.

"Arrrggh, someone will have to get out and push the boat into deeper water!" says Whippy, again in pirate-talk.

Puff gets out and calls to Crane, "C'mon, give me a hand."

"Okay, okay, the two of you get out and push," Whippy orders.

Crane and Puff push the boat out a little and jump back in. Puff's pants somehow get caught on the edge of the boat. "Hey! I'm stuck! I can't get loose!"

Kilowatts and PJ's grab Puff by the back of the pants and pull on him, but he's still stuck. They pull again, this time lifting him straight up in the air, almost pulling his pants off. Puff squirms around in midair. "Let me down! Let go!"

They look at each other, and then drop him. He rolls and hits his head on one of the barrel seats. "Ouch! It really hurts! Thanks a lot!"

"Well, you said, 'Let go'!"

Puff rubs his head and grumpily sits on one of the barrel seats closest to Whippy, near the keel.

They start to row. The boys on the right side of the boat row forward while the left-side boys row backward. They all row harder and harder, causing the boat to slowly spin. Whippy slaps his forehead in frustration. "Row the other way!"

They all reverse and start turning the boat in the other direction. Now Whippy is totally flustered. "No, no! Everybody row in the same direction!"

They all row backward, causing the boat to run aground. Whippy rubs his face and looks to the sky, as if for an answer. "Why me? Row, mates! Row forward!"

They row as hard as they can, but the boat won't move. Crane climbs out. "I guess it's get out and push again."

Puff follows him. "We've got to get it out in deeper water."

They push and push until finally the boat jerks loose and floats toward deeper water. A few swim strokes to the boat, and they both jump into it. Puff quietly admonishes the crew. "Let's all try to row in the same direction and move the boat forward for a change."

"Okay, Puffy," Big C answers with his usual flair.

His arrogance gets to Puff. "Don't call me Puffy."

Big C cannot control his impulses to irritate Puff a little more. "Okay, I won't call you Puffy. 'Puffy' won't be uttered from my lips again. I mean, I won't even speak the word 'Puffy' again. It just won't be spoken again, because 'Puffy' isn't what you like."

Puff groans and wishes Big C would just zip his lip.

"Never again will I call you—"

"Shut up, Ceee!" Puff hollers, losing his cool.

*   *   *   *

The rowing has proven that working together moves the boat where they want it to go. They have reached the middle of the lake, and the river outlet is in sight. "Ahoy, laddies!" Whippy shouts. "Thar flows the river!"

They quickly approach the mouth of the river. "It'll be a lot harder to control the boat rowing out of the river when we come back," Big C reasons.

PJ's thinks for a moment. "Huh? Oh, right, yup. I remember, back in my younger days I went down the Amazon River. There were these very dangerous…"

Crane groans as the other boys wave PJ's off. "I suppose you made yourself appear there with your magic? Ha, ha!"

"Peons!" PJ's retorts.

Puff notices a breeze. "Let the sail down. We'll use some wind power."

Whippy and Crane stand up and untie the sail, which has a wood limb rolled up in it to hold the bottom tight. As it unrolls, it hits Big C on the head. "Ouch! Watch it!"

Everyone laughs. "Peons!" says Big C.

As the sail fills with air, the boat effortlessly glides them on their way. A little while later, where the river is about one hundred feet wide, the boys see Tall Tree and Brown Cow camped along the bank. They wave, and Puff hollers out, "How!"

"How!" Brown Cow hollers back.

Tall Tree is frowning at Brown Cow. "Is that all you can say?"

Brown Cow thinks for a second, waves back at the boys, and calls out, "How now! I Brown Cow!" He looks up at Tall Tree and gives him a big Cheshire-cat grin.

Tall Tree just shakes his head. "In your own word…Ugh! What else to say?"

Chapter 76

Heading Back Home, or It Feels Better to Feel Better

It is such a perfect day no one notices how much time has passed. The scenery is so beautiful—flowers, trees, the sun bright and warm, even some fairies flying around from time to time.

"Let's go ashore for awhile and take a little rest," suggests Aky, who is getting tired.

Puff turns the boat toward shore. "Good idea. We can have a snack and appreciate the beauty all around, and each other, even."

Ambo agrees. "We are a family. We are our happy thought."

"I don't know," says Okydoky quietly. "I don't trust certain people here."

Ambo is taken aback by Okydoky's comment. "Like who?"

Okydoky looks around. "Can't say, but he's lazy and dumb."

Ambo is shocked. "What a terrible thing to say! I don't know any one of us that is lazy and dumb!"

"Well, there is!"

Ambo is annoyed. "I think you need to talk to whoever it is and get it fixed."

Okydoky turns away, stares at Tain, and mumbles, "Don't trust him."

Tain is puzzled by Okydoky's weird stare.

The Rascals are happy as they begin to sing their theme song—except for Okydoky. Puff notices he is not having fun. "You okay, Oky?" He leans over to Tain. "We always have fun here. I've never seen anyone upset before like Oky. What's going on?"

Tain looks over at Oky. "Why do you keep giving me that bad look?"

"Something I did or said?" Oky rudely answers.

"What do you want? Y'all just dumb and lazy."

Tain whispers to Puff, "That's strange, not like Oky at all. Guess I'll have to talk to him when we get back."

*   *   *   *

The bow of the boat settles in the sand, and the boys get out one by one. Aky leaps out, causing the boat to teeter. Oky tries to get out, but the boat is still rocking, and it tips just enough to throw him into the water. Tain reaches out to help him, but Okydoky pulls back. "Don't need no help from y'all!"

Puff is fed up. "What is wrong with you, Okydoky? You aren't having a good time, and you're acting strange. Better get it out in the air before it makes you sick or something."

Oky just grunts as he wades closer to shore. Crane pipes up, "Oky, you're making all of us miserable with your attitude. I know you should be having a good time, but you're not! What is wrong with you?"

Oky, still in the water, looks at Tain and points at him. "Yea, okay, then. It's him. He's the one."

Tain can't believe what he's hearing. "What are you talking about? What did I ever do to you?"

Okydoky puts his hands on his hips and cocks his head in an ugly sort of way. "Tain was supposed to help me with the chores for the last week, but he didn't help at all! He made me do it all! He is dumb and lazy!"

Puff, remembering, slaps his forehead. "You gotta be kidding me! I asked Tain to do something else. Aky was supposed to help you. I told Crane to tell him."

Crane lowers his head, a little embarrassed. "I forgot."

"You mean you been holding the mad in all this time over that?" Puff says to Okydoky.

Crane, who lives by a passage he once heard, quotes it: " 'Don't let the sun go down on your anger.' It's not good for you or anyone else."

Okydoky looks over at Tain. "I'm sorry, Tain. Guess I was wrong about you all."

Tain holds out his hand to Okydoky. "If you're big enough to admit you were wrong, I guess I'm big enough to accept your apology."

The boys shake hands and hug each other. Okydoky smiles. "It sure feels better to feel better."

"Holding in bad feelings just is no fun," offers Crane with a smile.

"We'd better set sail for home," says Tain, pointing his thumb in back of him. "Maybe we didn't get to the end, but we sure have had an interesting time."

Okydoky looks around at the beautiful scenery for the first time. "Sho' am pretty down this way."

"We've never been this far before," Aky chimes in. "Wonder what it's like down farther?"

Okydoky puts his arm around Tain. "Don't know, but we can find out together next time."

All yell, "BANGARANG!" and begin to sing as they climb into the boat.

*   *   *   *

The sun is beginning its descent as evening approaches. Whippy points to it. "I think it's getting late. We'd better hurry back before it gets too dark."

The boys start rowing all together to turn the boat around, but they row so hard they spin in a circle. "Everyone, stop rowing!" Puff hollers.

All oars halt instantly. The boat gently turns itself completely around, and they are headed back. The boys row in unison but seem to struggle against the river. Puff realizes they are fighting the sail. "Shouldn't we roll the sail back up?"

Whippy agrees. "Up with the sail, mates."

Crane and Big C tie the sail up, and they are on their way.

As they cruise toward the lake, Puff makes his way to the back of the boat and peers over the edge. "A fish! I think I see a fish!"

The boys all jump up to see, but in their excitement accidentally knock Puff overboard into the water. "Everyone, sit down!" Whippy hollers.

Crane and Big C reach over the edge of the boat to grab Puff and pull him in, but he rejects their help. "I'll get back in myself."

"Okay, Puffy, we're just here to help."

"Didn't I tell you not to call me that anymore, C?"

"Okay, I won't call you Puffy," Big C laughs. " 'Puffy' won't be uttered from my lips again. I mean I won't even speak the word 'Puffy' again. It just won't be spoken again, because 'Puffy' isn't what you like."

"Shut up, Ceeee!" all the boys shout.

Puff is totally annoyed. As he tries to climb back into the boat by himself, his pants get caught and he is stuck. Crane remembers Puff being stuck the same way at the beginning of this adventure. "C, let's pull him straight up again."

As they do, Puff is jerked loose, and he flies straight up and into the boat and once again lands on his head. He is wet and frustrated as he heads toward Whippy, who is laughing under his breath, "Twice is more funnierest than once."

Puff hears Whippy but is too miffed to respond.

The sun sets further as the boat reaches its original launch site. The lake is peaceful, and the friendly sound of the waterfall welcomes them back. "Great rowing, laddies," Puff says. "Let's get to shore."

Just before they reach shore, the boat hits bottom again. Crane and Big C already know the routine and get out to pull the vessel to shore. Everyone lands on shore, safe and sound. The boat is secure and ready for the next trip.

"That was an adventure," PJ's says, "but next time let's start earlier and go farther."

"Sounds good to me, but let's go back and eat," Crane says. "I'm starving."

The smell of good food and baked goodies greets the boys as they approach home. They see that everyone else is already seated around the table, where everything from cakes to cocoa, roasted turkey and pork, cheese and tasty bread is neatly laid out. Imagination is a wonderful thing, and in Neverland, Tinker Bell can conjure up the best of feasts for this hungry crew.

When all are seated, Whippy offers a prayer: "Thank you, Lord, for this food and giving it to us."

Crane lifts his cocoa mug. "Amen! Now let's eat!"

They all dig in.

Hawkins raises her mug. "I love my Po Po."

Goatee sits up like a dog, pawing the air, begging for scraps. Sneezer laughs and flips Goatee a broccoli head. Just like a dog, he catches it in his mouth. His tail wags as he carries it off to enjoy this tasty tidbit.

As they all finish eating, they stretch, burp, rub their bellies, and head for their beds. Several little lights flicker throughout their huge monkey-pod treehouse and go out one by one as the Rascals turn in for the night. A full moon and bright stars light up the night sky. From time to time a night-bird calls, or fireflies float around in the dark.

<h1 style="text-align:center">Chapter 77</h1>

<h1 style="text-align:center">Pirate Aggravation</h1>

The next day after lunch, the Rascals stand around the table, trying to decide on the day's adventure. Aky waves his hand in the air. "Let's go fly our kite."

After a few moments, Ambo raises her hand. "No, let's have relay races."

Okydoky stands up on the bench. "Know wat I'd lak to do? Why I'd lak to go chase some of dem wabbits we seen over yonda."

Big C can't resist: " 'Wabbits'? What's a 'wabbit'? I believe they are called rabbits. Is that what you mean? Rabbits?"

Okydoky frowns a little, and with his very obvious drawl speaks slowly and clearly: "Dat's exactly wat ah said. Wabbits."

Big C is about to comment, but when he notices Oky chewing on a piece of straw, he gives up, knowing Oky is from the Deep South. "Okay, Oky. Okay."

"Now look heah, Big C. Y'all know ma name is Okydoky, doesn't you? So if'n y'all don't mind, Okydoky'll suit me fine."

Whippy takes charge. "We can't all do what everyone wants to. We'll have to decide on one thing."

"Ya, let's have relay races!" says Aky, in accord with Ambo.

"Oh, no," groans Whippy, "not that, Ambo! You always win the relay races. Let's figure out an adventure for today."

Aky volunteers. "I know, I know. Let's go get us some aggravation!"

"Aggravation?" wonders Big C out loud. "Your idea is aggravating enough! Whoever heard of getting some aggravation?"

"What do you mean by aggravation?" Whippy asks.

Squinting and raising an eyebrow, Aky looks around at everyone. "Let's go to the village today and aggravate some pirates."

Everyone knows just what he is thinking, and they all agree.

Big C raises his finger. "This is the first time something that didn't make sense…makes sense!"

Whippy looks over at Puff and shrugs his shoulders. "Huh?"

Puff laughs. "Yeah, let's all start thinking up some ideas that'll annoy the pirates and meet back here!"

Whippy grins from ear to ear, delighted with the idea. "And see who wants to go!"

Everyone is heading in different directions. Some are rounding up anyone else who may want to join them. Others have formed small groups and are already making plans. It doesn't take long, only about ten minutes, as this is one of their favorite adventures—usually to the pirates' chagrin.

Puff, Crane, Big C, and Kilowatts rejoin the rest of the Rascals at the table. "We have our plans figured out. How about the rest of you?"

All share their ideas and make ready for their adventure: "Pirate aggravation."

The table fills with buckets and ropes, small tools in a sack, a homemade gorilla mask, and a sack of flour and lanterns. It is an odd array of items, but all with a purpose.

All shout, "BANGARANG!" as they start their hike to the village.

Goatee tags along after them. Bangarangatang joins the group, hitching a ride on Goatee's back. He doesn't seem to mind his passenger at first, until he can't scratch the itch, so to speak. He is annoyed because the monkey's tail is tickling his back. After tolerating it for a little while longer, Goatee jumps around, shakes like a dog after a swim in the lake, and dumps Bangarangatang off. The monkey screeches, purses his lips at Goatee, and scampers up into the trees, following the Rascals from above.

As they near the village, they slow down and are very quiet. Puff whispers to Crane, "I'll bet our idea is the best!"

Crane forgets to whisper. "Yup, I'm sure it is!"

Puff puts his finger to his lips. Crane nods his head.

At the edge of the forest they can see the small village. All is calm; not many pirates are wandering about. Whippy quietly gathers everyone around. "This is going to be great fun, so let's all work our 'pirate aggravation' plans. But remember, be careful."

It is almost dusk as each group heads in a different direction into the village, some remaining at the forest edge. The Rascals are not easily seen in the shadows and know where to hide as they approach their targets. Okydoky seems to lollygag along, watching Bangarangatang up in the trees. Ambo and Aky grab Oky and pull him along. "Come on, don't be a slowpoke," Aky whispers. "We gotta move faster."

As the Rascals head toward the tavern, Bangarangatang jumps out of the trees and follows close behind them. Sneezer, Tain and Whippy take another direction, inching their way down toward the docks. Big C, Kilowatts, Puff and Crane head toward the shops. They are all set to embark on "pirate aggravation."

Chapter 78

The Tavern's Tiny Gorilla
or, "The Gerrrilla"

ky, Ambo and Oky are out of sight, hiding just off the corner of the tavern's large-paned window. Ambo pokes her head around and peeks in. She sees just enough, then scoots back to report to the others, "The place is full."

Inside the tavern are several pirates, barmaids and other odd sorts, all drinking grog and laughing loudly. A big pot of simmering stew hangs on the hearth of the huge rock fireplace. Aky checks the gorilla mask and whispers, "We all know what to do, right? And be careful!"

They all silently nod their heads in agreement. Oky grins with excitement. "This is gonna be a lot of fun."

Bang tilts his head sideways and flashes a big toothy grin as he watches Aky don the gorilla mask. Ambo peeks through the window again. She has to duck back a few times so as not to be seen. She waits to give the signal. A barmaid is carrying a large tray of hot stew to one of the tables facing the window. Just as she dips to serve them, Ambo whispers, "Now."

Oky grunts and growls like a gorilla. Aky sticks his masked head up in the window and bobs around, with only his gorilla face showing in the window.

The barmaid, balancing a tray of bowls filled with hot stew, hears the commotion outside. "Them darn dogs in the garbage again." She looks up toward the window and sees a quick flash of the gorilla face, but only for a second. She shakes her head in disbelief and mutters, "I must need eyeglasses!"

Aky pops up again. She points to the window as she shrieks. In the excitement of the moment she dumps half of the bowls of hot stew on the table. Some land on a pirate. He jumps up, screaming, knocking the tray from her hand, and sending the other half of the bowls into the air. Hot stew is flying everywhere, inciting much confusion. Pirates yell and bound around with hot stew burning them and a gorilla in the window.

The barmaid tries to back away from the table, but her foot slips on the stew-soaked floor, and she lands on her bum. Dazed and shocked, she mutters, "It's not possible! There can't be a gorilla in the window!" The scene is total chaos. What a sight, seeing the barmaid planted in the stew, the tray on the floor, not too far from where she landed.

Aky pops his gorilla face up one more time. The barmaid, seeing it again, points to the window and screams out, "A gorilla, I tell ya! I seen a gorilla in the window!"

Squealing and laughing with delight, Aky and the others run toward the forest, stopping safely at the edge, hidden from the tavern, watching the chaos. Bangarangatang still sits under the window, waiting. A pirate looks out the window to check what was out there. "Thar ain't nothin' heah."

The barmaid is really upset. "There was a gorilla, I tell ya, and don't you tell me there weren't!" she screeches. "I know a gorilla when I see one!"

Knowing the barmaid's temperament, the pirate cautiously approaches her to help her up off the floor. "Okay missy, okay. I'm gonna go take a look see out thar." He helps her up, calms her down, and walks out the door to see what he can see.

Bangarangatang screeches, growls like a gorilla as he flips backwards, and hops up and down. The pirate is startled as he watches the monkey in disbelief. With an exploding "Blaaah!" he bursts out in uncontrollable laughter and stumbles back inside the door. He is laughing so hard he can hardly stand. "Ha, ha, ha, you... Ha, ha, everyone, you... Ha, ha, gotta see these pop, hee-hee, popping peepers, ha, ha, ha!"

The pirates run to the door, pushing each other out of the way to get outside. Bangarangatang is doing his whole act to the delight of the pirates, who can't contain themselves, laughing hysterically and hanging all over each other. "Wee-hee-hee, better get outta here," laughs one of them. "This here guerrilla, 'ees gonna get us. Ba-ha-ha."

"The eyes, the eyes, them are some big eyes, hee-hee," laughs another. "'Ees a scary little monster, 'ee is, ha-ha, careful mates, sure 'ees gonna get us."

Bangarangatang, having jumped around, growls and screeches just enough, jumps in the air, spins around, and heads off, running full speed toward the forest. The three Rascals watch from their location and head deeper into the woods. Reaching its safety, they laugh and roll on the ground, loving every minute of their rollicking adventure.

Aky catches his breath, sits up and holds his tummy. "That was just too much. Too much muchness." His laughter is so contagious everyone else bursts out once again.

Bangarangatang reaches the forest and goes directly to Ambo, who laughs and pets him. "Good job, Bang. That was great fun."

The monkey shows off a little more, enjoying the moment.

"Wow, even pirates have a sense of humor!" Ambo laughs.

Chapter 79

The Trip-Trap Rope

Whippy, Tain and Sneezer are hiding behind some barrels by one of the shops. Only a few pirates hang around the dock, but enough to create some action. Further down the dock are wooden steps to the pier below.

Knowing the dock well, Whippy points to them. "Now, see those steps over there, the ones leading down to the pier?"

Sneezer and Tain nod their heads. "Let's make our way over there, but be careful," Tain says.

Moving quietly and swiftly, unnoticed by the pirates, they reach the steps and climb down, checking behind them to be sure no one sees them. Tain points to a pole sticking up from the pier a few feet to the left of the steps. "We can tie the rope over there," he whispers. "It's the perfect spot."

He sneaks toward the pole, hiding behind a nearby barrel for a moment, making sure the coast is clear. When he's sure it's safe, he leaves the barrel and heads for the pole to tie the rope. To the right of the steps are two barrels. Whippy grabs the other end of the rope and hides behind the first barrel. Sneezer sneaks down the last of the steps, then runs and hides behind the second barrel. Tain waits until all of the boys are settled, then quickly makes his way over to them.

They are very quiet as they wait for a victim or more to fall prey to their rope trap. Tain grins and looks things over. "This will be great fun. Can't wait to see a pirate fall into the water."

Whippy is excited. "All we have to do is pull the rope at just the right time."

Sneezer is laughing quietly. "Yeah, and we can call it a Pirate Waterfall!"

They are all chuckling when suddenly they hear footsteps coming toward them. Is the wait over? Is the action about to begin? Whippy grabs the rope, ready to pull. The footsteps are from three drunken pirates. One is big and burly, the second quite average in size, the third short and slight—"Shorty" by name, but nonetheless just as drunk. They stagger toward the steps, still lifting their rum mugs to their ugly mugs, totally oblivious of what's to come.

Watching them approach, Tain whispers, "I can see them from here. You two yank the rope hard when I give the signal."

As the pirates near, Sneezer lets out a big sneeze. Tain, acting quickly, plants his hand over Sneezer's mouth, but possibly too late. The big burly pirate, his arms stretching out to stop the other two, halts and looks around. "That sounded like a sneeze to me! Which one of you sneezed?"

The pirates shrug their shoulders. The average-sized one, after thinking for a moment, suggests, "We didn't sneeze. Maybe you sneezed?"

The big, burly one shakes his head. "Think I ought to know if it were me. Just pipe down. See if ye hear anything."

All three stand as motionless as drunken pirates can, listening for another sneeze. Hearing nothing more, they continue on their way, staggering toward the steps. They stop at the top of the steps and look down, as if atop a very high mountain. Drunk and swaying a bit, the big, burly pirate warns, "Gotta make it down these steps, mates."

The short, slight pirate takes the lead. Watching his feet, he puts his foot down on the first step.

"Watch yer footing," says the big, burly one. "Steady as ye go. Can't stumble, or you'll be wettin' yer mug in the briny."

"Argh!" spews the short, slight pirate indignantly. "I ain't that drunk, matey."

The other two laugh as they watch him wobble his way down. Safe at the bottom of the steps, he confidently calls out, "Come on now, mates! It's a piece of cake! No problem at all!"

The others unsteadily make their way down. "We be thar!" says the big, burly one. "Hold yer mug."

Shorty holds up his mug. "Got it right here." Taking a big gulp, he spouts out, "My mug in my mug! Harrr."

With perfect timing, Tain gives the signal, the rope pulls tight, and both pirates trip over the rope and tumble forward. The big, burly one tumbles headlong, hitting the pier face-first, as Shorty, feet flying over his head, lands on top of him and rolls into the average-sized pirate, causing both to fall off the pier and into the briny.

The big, burly pirate, still too drunk to balance himself, looks up, dazed and confused. He wobbles very, very closely to the edge of the pier. Looking back up the steps, he sees the rope and hears the kids laughing from behind the barrels. Still staggering, he calls out, "I see you Rascal kids!" No sooner do those words come out of his mouth than he falls over into the water, plopping right on top of the first pirate coming up for air.

Three drunken pirates are in the briny, and three Rascals are laughing as they run away. Tain yells out a tune, "Three drunken pirates in the briny! They are wet from head to hinny. Haaa!" The boys all laugh as they dart to safety.

Quickly sobering up from the salty water, the three pirates swim the short way back to the pier, boost one another up, and manage to get back up onto the dock. Soaking wet and angry, they start up the steps, looking for the kids. The big, burly pirate swears an oath: "We're gonna get you kids for this!"

Whippy, Tain and Sneezer are long gone, having taken off between the buildings and headed for the forest. The Rascals run, laughing and frolicking, along the way. Once back to the safety of the forest they head up the trail to their agreed meeting place.

Chapter 80

Floury Pirates

Big C, Kilowatts, Puff, and Crane are hiding in the alley between two of the shops. The shadows hide them from view. Puff points out a particular shop. "There! That shop over there would work perfectly."

The eave of the structure extends over the walkway in front of the shop. A few barrels rest against the wall. The empty hooks that display the goods during the day now look odd in the dim light. Big C points to the entrance. "That beam under the eaves over the door is perfect. We can hide around in the alley and make this work."

The boys sneak over to the other side of the alley with a bucket, a bag of flour, and a rope. Kilowatts quickly dumps the flour into the bucket as Big C uses his hands to explain to Crane how to run the rope up and over the beam to pull off this caper.

Crane is careful not to be seen as he sneaks to the front of the shop, carrying the bucket and rope. Inside, the owner and a clerk are at the back, having a drink together as they go over the receipts for the day. Crane quietly pulls a barrel over to the door, climbs up on it, and sets the bucket onto the beam. He quickly secures the rope and runs it along the beam through one of the hooks and over to Puff, who grabs the rope and takes it into the alley. Crane quickly and quietly puts the barrel back and joins the others. Kilowatts watches the door, but no one comes out yet.

They wait, and it is getting late, but Crane has an idea. He picks up a rock, shows it to the boys, and points at the door. They all nod in understanding, but Puff warns, "Really, be careful. Don't get caught."

Everyone is ready as Crane runs to the door and throws the rock against it, making just enough noise to get the attention of the shop owner and the clerk. Hearing the clatter, they go quickly to the door. The owner throws it open, just in time to see Crane running away. A couple of pirates are walking across the street. The owner runs out, yelling, "Hey, stop that kid! That Rascal is getting away!" The pirates run toward the owner to see what the clamor is all about. "No, not me!" he says, pointing into the dark. "That kid that's getting away!"

By the time the pirates understand, Crane is out of sight and nowhere to be found. "We see nothing in the streets, mate," says one of the pirates. The owner, grateful anyway, invites them in for a drink. They look at each other, and one eyes the owner with a grin. "We can do that."

"Follow me to the back of the shop."

"Those meddling forest kids. We should thank them, though, for the drink, harrr."

Crane is now with the others, hiding in the shadows of the alley, waiting for the right moment. Puff holds the rope tight, and just as the pirates pass under the beam, he yanks it good and hard. The flour dumps on both pirates at the same time, and the empty bucket hits one of them on the head.

"Oww! Argh!"

Flour is piled all over them. The shop owner hears the noise and goes back out the door. He sees the floury pirates and bursts out in laughter. But this is no joke to the pirates, who shake their fists in the air. "One of these days we'll get you Rascals, and that'll be the end of you!" shouts one.

The kids hear that threat as they dash toward the forest and out of sight, laughing and mocking the pirates along the way. Almost out of breath, Puff gasps, "Now that's what I call flour makin' pirates sour! Harr, harr, harr!"

Chapter 81

Homeward Bound

The path is dark now, and the Rascals are glad they brought their lanterns. Tinker Bell meets them at the agreed place along the path. "I thought you Rascals would've been back before dark, but the look on your faces tells me you have amazing adventures to share when we get home."

Laughter can be heard as Crane, Big C, Puff, and Kilowatts catch up. Puff grins from ear to ear as he holds his lantern high, lighting up everyone's faces and accenting their expressions of delight. Aky, excited, wants to hear all about "Flour makin' 'em sour," but Big C puts up his finger. "We will give an exact account and complete description of our adventures when we get home."

Ambo scrunches up her face and shakes her head, interpreting Big C's words as, "In other words, can't wait to tell you all about it."

As they head home they all share bits and parts of their stories, making the homeward trip fun and full of laughter. Tinker Bell goes ahead of the Rascals. "I'll see to dinner. Everyone must be starving after such great adventures."

They return to the treehouse, drop their gear and head for the table. Goatee and Bangarangatang are already back. The monkey is on the table, tossing pieces of food down to Goatee. "Have you ever seen a goat that sits up, front legs in the air, like a dog begging for table scraps?" Pinner asks humorously.

Indeed, the Rascals are all very hungry, and in no time the food is gone.

Only hot cocoa and cakes remain as they begin to share the details of each adventure while eating cake and drinking Po Po. Sharing their stories is almost as much fun as the event itself.

After Puff shares his share of the adventure, Crane laughs and hollers, "We got pirate sour flour power!"

Ambo finishes the Tavern Tiny Gorilla adventure with, "Argh, mateys, we got a big mean grrrr-rilla, too! Ha, ha!"

Bangarangatang hams it up a bit as he jumps up and down, back-flips, and chatters and growls like a "grrrr-rilla."

Finally, Whippy, Tain, and Sneezer share their stories of the Trip-Trap Rope and the drunken pirates' dip in the briny. Shadows dance around as the lanterns flicker.

The Rascals have had a wonderful journey of excitement and adventures. It's been a very long day, and the hour is late. Puff yawns and stretches. "I don't know about anyone else, but I'm tired and hittin' the hay."

"I'm gonna be one of them thar hay-hitters, too," Oky adds.

Tinker Bell flies down and around the Rascals and reminds them, "Off with all of you now. You'll need to be rested up for tomorrow's great adventure. Good night, you Neverland Rascals."

They all head to their beds. Voices are heard as they nestle in: "'Night, Tinker Bell. 'Night, Rascals. 'Night, Neverland."

Chapter 82

The Talent Show

The Rascals are hanging around the treehouse about midday, looking at each other, wondering what to do next. "What do you want to do?" Tain asks.

"I don't know," Hawkins replies. "What do you want to do?"

"I don't know wha… Wait, we're not doing that again!"

Kilowatts holds one hand on his chest and sticks his arm out. "I'll sing for ya."

"No, no, that's okay," Tain says abruptly.

Hawkins dances around, up and down. "I can dance and sing!"

Puff rubs his chin. "This gives me an idea. Let's have a talent show."

They all look at each other. Then, one at a time, they say, "Yeah!"

"Let's have a prize for the winner who has the most votes," Whippy says. "Anyone have any ideas for a prize?"

Big C raises his finger. "The winner could get a dictionary."

"We don't even have one," says Aky, "but how about an extra ride in the barrel?"

"How about the winner gets to be the king or queen for the day?" Whippy proposes with authority. "Everyone has to serve them."

"BANGARANG!" they all shout.

Whippy lifts his finger, aping Big C. "Okay then, let's get started and build a stage."

They dig out the side of the hill for the floor, put up posts for the curtains, tie a rope from post to post, and hang big blankets from the rope. The stage is finished by evening. They set the date of their talent show for the next day and go to the table to eat. Hawkins picks up some food but changes her mind: "I'm too tired to food-fight."

So, they eat, go to bed, and fall asleep while looking up at the beautiful stars and colorful mist in the air created by the shimmering moon off the turquoise water.

*　*　*　*

The next morning, all of the Rascals get ready for the show. They set stumps and logs for chairs to sit on. The curtain is connected in the middle with a rope so it can be pulled back when each act is ready. They all sit, waiting their turns.

Whippy comes on stage and greets them like a circus announcer. "Hear, hear! We have come together to find the best talent Neverland has to offer! You each vote for someone, and it can't be yourself!"

Holding his homemade cane, he sings a little song:

> *Here we are at the show!*
>
> *The best is here, don't you know!*
>
> *Sing and dance on the stage!*
>
> *You'll have fun before you go!*
>
> *What a sight for you to see,*
>
> *The best for you, the best for me!*
>
> *The winner will be king or queen.*

It may be he, it may be she.

On with the show we go!

After his poem Whippy announces, "Ladies and gents! For our first act, be prepared to engage your brain. The Big C recites a poem, and recites it not in vain!"

Big C begins:

I love the stars, I love the moon,

I love them when they shine in June.

I love the sun, I love the sky,

I love the tears that it cries.

Big C walks over to the side of the stage as he recites. When just about finished, he grabs the curtain to lean on it. Just as sure as the Big C stands for 'curse,' he pulls down the cloth and reveals other kids getting ready. The kids all laugh and point at him.

Whippy comes out and holds up his hands. "Let's give a big hand to Big C!"

The kids clap and holler as others remount the curtain. One kid is bending over, grabbing something just as he sneezes. Goatee hears him, charges at him, and butts him off the stage. The goat jumps up and down to celebrate. The kids again all point and laugh. Kilowatts comes out and grabs Goatee.

Whippy introduces the next performer: "The next act is very hot. You could call him Kilowatts."

The kids laugh again. The curtain is pulled back, and there stands

Kilowatts. He starts to sing, but just then Goatee chases another kid across the stage. The kids all laugh and clap. One stands up and says, "Goatee is the best act! Ha!"

Kilowatts, irritated, starts again: "O sole mio!" Goatee chases the same kid back across the stage. They disappear behind the curtain, and the kid climbs up a tree while the goat stands there, grunting, puffing and pawing the ground. The kids are rolling off their seats in laughter. Whippy comes out, calms them down, and says to Kilowatts, "Go ahead."

"O sole mio!" Kilowatts continues while Goatee hides behind a tree, looking around, waiting for the kid to come down. He climbs down the tree, walks over toward the stage, and watches from behind the curtain. Out of nowhere, the goat jumps out after him, and they are off again across the floor while Kilowatts is trying to sing.

Finally fed up with this fracas, Kilowatts stomps his foot and storms off the stage. Loud banging and dust emerges from around the curtain, followed by a big, blood-curdling "Baaaa!" Goatee runs across the stage like a dog, his butt tucked in, hollering, "Arghr! Arghr! Arghr!"

Out from behind the curtain and onto the stage comes Hawkins. With both fists doubled up and one up in the air, she hollers, "I'll rip your lip!"

All the kids stand up, holler and clap. One yells, "BANGARANG, Hawkins!"

She walks off the stage with both hands straight down and clinched fists. The curtain comes together, and Whippy walks out with his hands in the air. "Settle down! Settle down! We need to get to our next act! The next act is great indeed, and is extraordinary beyond your dream! I introduce Ambo!"

Pinner stands up. "You gonna do flips with Bangarangatang…haaa!"

The kids know Ambo is very athletic, so they get a big kick out of what Pinner is saying, and they holler and clap. Ambo walks out and has a bad feeling about doing her act. She remembers the rejection she felt when they were left out on the snowy street of the orphanage. No one wanted them. How terrible for a kid. But she is very strong, smart, and determined. She looks over to the side of the stage and motions for someone to come out. Out walks Hawkins. The kids applaud. Hawkins stands there on guard for Goatee. Ambo starts singing, and everyone is so quiet. Her voice is like an angel.

Unknown to Ambo, Tinker Bell has gathered many fairies hiding in the trees. Each has an instrument, and they start playing one at a time until they are playing a song together. Not knowing where the music is coming from, the kids all look around but see and hear nothing but beautiful music.

Living in Neverland is just like a dream.

Everywhere you look is a beautiful scene.

Adventures and fun or lay in the sun,

Living in Neverland is just like a dream.

Living in Neverland is a wonderful place.

Never a frown, never feel down, or a long face.

We'll never grow up while Po Po we sup.

Living in Neverland is just like a dream.

Mystical trees so high, flowers that glow below,

Sparkling light on the clouds from a rainbow,

Colors beyond anything that we ever knew.

Neverland glitters, shines and shimmers,

Neverland glows.

Living in Neverland—what a wonderful place!

Never a frown, never feel down, or a long face.

We'll never grow up while Po Po we sup.

Living in Neverland is just like a dream.

Living in Neverland is just like a dream.

When she is done, they are all just sitting there and staring. She thinks once again she has been rejected and they don't like her as she sadly walks off. Just then they all jump up and clap and holler, "More! More!"

Tears fill Ambo's eyes as she waves and walks off-stage. She doesn't care about winning, just not being rejected again. She cares so much about her Rascal family. Still wondering where the music came from, Ambo looks around but sees nothing.

Tinker Bell keeps the secret of the music to herself, at least for now.

The curtain comes down. Out comes Whippy again, cane in hand. "Let us amaze you with a trick and treat. Amazing PJ's is here with a magic feat."

Out walks PJ's with a magic wand in his hand. "The amazing PJ's will amaze you with amazing feats of magic! You will be amazed!"

Once again, Pinner stands up. "I think your brain is in a maze! Ha, ha, ha!"

The kids all laugh. PJ's just says, "Harrumph! Let me demonstrate. I have this wand and this egg. I will wave the wand over the egg, and it will disappear."

Another kid rises. "Yeah, right!"

"Be still, peon!" He starts to wave his wand over the egg, but nothing happens. The kids laugh again. Pinner stands. "I don't think I can take anymore! My stomach is hurting from the laughing! Haaa!"

PJ's points his wand right at Pinner. "Peon!" He shakes it harder over the egg. Nothing happens.

Another kid stands up. "Try two hands!"

Then PJ's grips the wand and shakes it as if he is trying to kill it. With a flash of light the wand disappears, and the egg is still there. The kids all gasp. PJ's, dumbfounded as the others, just says, "Meant to do that." Taking advantage of the situation, he walks off stage and points again to Pinner, but, trying to be nice, says nothing. All the kids just sit there with their mouths open.

Unbeknownst to anyone, Goatee is getting into a big box behind the stage and lying down inside. He is just about asleep as the top falls shut.

PJ's is back on stage with more confidence: "The next trick will be making my assistant disappear."

Two kids bring out a big wooden box and set it down. One says, "This is one heavy box," as he wipes his brow and they walk off.

"I will have my assistant climb into the box," PJ's says. "I will count to three, and then open the box, and she will be gone. Hopefully still in Neverland. Will my assistant please assist me."

Out comes Ambo, wearing a Tinker Bell type of costume, and walks up to the box. PJ's walks over to it and says he has to make some magic over it. All the kids watch with big eyes open in wonder. "Now is the time for your amazement. Ambo, open the box and climb in."

She does, and out jumps Goatee. All of the kids jump up and run for cover. The goat darts from side to side on the stage. Out from the right side comes Hawkins, who growls and takes two steps forward. The goat's eyes pop, and he takes off in the other direction.

"Get 'im, Hawkins!" Pinner hollers.

Then out comes Whippy as the curtain closes. "Bring out all the acts so we can vote." All of the performers come out, line up and sing:

> *For your gracious time*
> *We leave you with this rhyme.*
> *Goodbye, so long, farewell.*
> *We hope you had some fun.*
> *Now we have to leave*
> *Like the setting sun.*

The kids all go behind the curtain, and the others clap and start to leave as the sun begins to set. At the table they gather to vote. It takes a while, but finally the tally is in: it's a tie between Ambo and PJ's. All are happy for the winners and congratulate them.

The sun's golden rays are sprinkled with rainbow colors. The rising moon mixes with the setting sun, creating wondrous mixtures of hues and sparkles on the water and in the air. The night-birds call quietly. Fairy lights in the forest fly hither and thither. Flowers glow in all shades and colors. Vines climb trees with glowing flowers. The silhouettes of the tops of the trees are dark against the colorful, sparkling starry sky.

Chapter 83

Down the River to Nowhere, Once Again

The next day, Tain and Ambo are inside the treehouse, but underground. It is a very large room with roots and rocks and plenty of room for all the kids. The extremely large monkey-pod tree looms high above the other trees of the forest and jungles. Tain sits in the large seat carved out of the rock and wood of the roots.

A large wooden burl table is before him; Ambo sits on it. They quietly look around at the beauty that surrounds them. Gems in the walls shimmer from the candles. Colors from the gems glow in the pool.

Ambo breaks the silence softly: "Everywhere we go, it is so beautiful… Tain… Do you remember where we came from?"

The question surprises Tain. "Came from? Err, I remember something— um, ahh—wait, I remember. Yes, actually I do, now that you mention it. That is where Thomas took care of us at the orphanage. I wonder whatever happened to all of the other kids."

Ambo points at Tain. "That is exactly what I was thinking. Ha!"

"That is why I said it. Ha!" Tain points back at Ambo.

Ambo looks around. "What a blessed life we live here in Neverland. How is it we were chosen out of all the others in the world?"

"Because we are all so good looking and extreeemely smart, ha!"

Again, they laugh. Then Ambo speaks a little more solemnly. "I remember something about my mother and father, but I'm not sure what it is. It comes in bits and pieces now and then."

Tain picks up Ambo's solemn tone. "I kinda have the same memory, Ambo. Maybe someday we can both remember more…someday."

Ambo stands up, twirls around with her arms outstretched, and enjoys the room of beauty and safety. "You know, it is so safe here at our home…and we have many great adventures, but have yet to go farther down the River to Nowhere."

Tain gazes at Ambo and pauses. "You know, you're right. So, let's do it!"

"Yeah, let's get 'em all together and decide who goes."

They climb up and out and ring the bell. Soon all Rascals surround the table. "Who rang the bell?" Crain asks.

Ambo raises her hand. "It was I, matey, and we have an announcement. Who wants to go down the River to Nowhere and see what is farther on?"

Everyone looks at each other for a moment, then starts raising hands one at a time. "You know that we can only take a few of us," says Tain, "but why don't we build another boat? We could even have races."

Big C points up in the air. "I can build a faster boat."

Puff glares at Big C. "Yeah, but will the boat float?"

Big C holds both hands up. "What do you expect, Puffy? I'll design another and better boat. Then we can all travel the River to Nowhere."

Ambo looks over at Big C. "We are going farther than ever before, so we need a safe and protective boat this time. We don't know what's down there."

Big C points up again. "The C knows what to do. Now, let's get at it."

The Rascals wait while Big C draws up the new plans. It takes him a long while. Getting antsy, Kilowatts walks up to Big C. "You about done yet, C?"

"Keep your britches on…almost done."

A short time later he announces, "Here is my drawing, ready to go." As he stands up, he trips and rips the plans in two. Everyone groans, but Big C places the halves of the drawing on the table together. As the kids all gather around, a few gasp, and even Ambo says, "Wow, very good, C! Can we even build this?"

Tain scans the drawing. "Yes, this is great, C, and yes, we can build this. We have a town full of everything we need! Ha."

The Rascals jump and cheer. "Down the river to Nowhere!" Pinner hollers. "Yeah! More adventures!" All the kids leap, holler and dance around in wild excitement.

"Let's all get some sleep," Tain declares. "We have to get to town tomorrow to get the supplies we don't have and get the boat built."

The Rascals wander off to their beds. The sun is setting with sparkling, shimmering colorful rays off the water, mixed with rainbow colors. The full yellow moon is rising and sending streaking rays scintillating on the water. The aquatic mix of sun and moon makes the water look almost like a rainbow. The mermaids jump out and make splashing sounds the Rascals can hear from the treehouse.

Off in the distance, night-birds call with almost surreal songs. The mystical trees silhouette high, and the flowers glow below—a beauty hard to put in words. Through the trees, flowers and greenery, the glow of a fairy floats by every now and then. It is a typical beautiful evening in Neverland—such a mystical, beautiful fantasy that one almost doesn't want to go to sleep.

Chapter 84:

Another Day, Another Trip

The next morning, the sun rises and sparkles once again on the water. The moon sets, leaving its own glimmers on the river. Seagulls call off in the distance as the Rascals start to wake.

Big C is up and ready, drawing in hand. "Time to build the boat of all boats!"

The kids slowly gather around one by one. Kilowatts says with his morning face, "Let's eat first." The others agree. In an instant they are all at table, and they close their eyes. Puff gives thanks for the food as each one imagines it. When they open their eyes, there it is—Neverfood.

They finish eating and are now ready for their next adventure. They gather in groups and head to town to get the necessary supplies. They have no problems, as they are very sneaky, and all get back home safe and sound. Big C gives each group a chore, and they hammer and cut their day away. At the end of the day the boat is complete.

Everyone stands back. All look at each other and marvel at their accomplishment. "Wow, and double wow!" says Hawkins in amazement. "I am ready!"

PJ's pats Big C on the back. "Gotta hand it to you, C, you have a great design. Hope it floats! Ha, ha!"

While the kids laugh, Tain looks over the situation. "One thing we forgot, C."

"I have forgotten nothing."

"Beggin' your pardon, matey," Tain responds in a mock-pirate voice, "but how we gonna get 'er down to the lake?"

Big C, realizing his dilemma, is somewhat embarrassed. "I know what to do."

Crane cocks his head to one side. "Yehhh? What?"

"Let me roll it through my mind a few times."

"You mess up again?" says Hawkins.

"Roll it around in your mind?" says Whippy, irked. "Roll it, pole it, you really blew it."

"Roll it, pole it!" says Big C. "That is how we get it to the lake. I knew it all along."

"Roll it, pole it, you got some o' dat der brain thang problems," says Okydoky.

Big C rolls his eyes. "We use round poles to roll it down to the lake. Push it on the round poles."

"Well, show us what you have in mind," says Puff skeptically.

"Get some round poles, and I'll show you how it works."

All the kids go in different directions. They manage to find enough poles, and Big C explains the procedure. They all take turns as they push the boat with the poles lying on the ground. One kid grabs a pole from behind the boat and puts it to the front. They do this over and over until they finally make their way to the lake. It is getting late by now, and they are all worn out.

Tain puts his finger in the air. "Let's start tomorrow, when we are rested."

All agree and head back home. Tain pauses to listen to the evening sounds of the waterfall and night-birds. You can almost hear the colors of the flowers, glowing brightly in the night. When he listens close and still, it seems he can hear their music. Each flower has a musical sound, and together they make a beautiful melody. Only some pay close enough attention at the right time to hear it.

As the Rascals prepare for bed, Whippy says to them, "We have a great adventure tomorrow. Let's bring all we need for an overnight camp out and for our protection. See you all in the morning."

Chapter 85

What Awaits Down the River

One by one the kids slowly show up at the lake after breakfast. Pinner looks over the two boats. "I get the big boat! Ha, ha!"

Whippy looks at Pinner and mimics Big C's air-pointing finger. "We will draw straws. Short straws go on the smaller boat."

After drawing their straws, they gather their supplies and load up the vessels. Just then, Tall Tree and Brown Cow show up. "Ugh," grunts Brown Cow.

Tall Tree slaps his forehead. "Ugh, ugh, ugh! That is an ugh-ly thing to say!"

"That not ugly." Brown Cow points at Tall Tree. "You ugly! Ha, ha!"

Tall Tree groans and then turns to the kids. "Where you go?"

Hawkins points to the river. "Down the River to great adventures."

Brown Cow shakes his head. "Bad idea. River go nowhere good."

"Have you been down the river?" Tain asks him. "If not, how do you know?"

Brown Cow rubs his chin. "Don't know how know, just know."

Ambo raises her hands. "We don't know, and that is the great adventure."

Tall Tree puts his hand on Brown Cow's shoulder. "Agree with Brown Cow. Very dangerous."

Brown Cow looks up at Tall Tree. "You agree with me?"

"Yupums."

Okydoky is tired of all the talk and eager to start the trip. "You all are quacking like ducks, and this heah day is getting a might sho'tah!"

With that the Rascals start climbing into the boats. As they head out onto the lake and toward the river, they sing the Neverland Rascals song and wave goodbye to Brown Cow and Tall Tree, who both shake their heads, turn and walk away into the forest.

Ambo looks over the supplies, "We have two days' worth of food and water. Let's see how far we get, and what will be the great adventure."

"BANGARANG!" all the kids holler.

The new boat, twice the size of the first, has higher sides and a much bigger sail. A rudder in the back guides it along the river. The front has an area for storage and weapons. The kids glide along, and after a while they pass the natives' camp on the shore. Just beyond the camp is the farthest they have gone so far.

"This is where we turned around last time," says Crane. "We are making history."

As they float down the river, the forest darkens from the dense trees. The flowers glow in the shadowy areas. Fairies fly around here and there. The trees appear more mystical as they loom over the river. Rays of sunlight beam through them, creating bright spots on the shore. The water sparkles where the sun shines. The tree shadows seem to move in the light.

The kids are getting nervous, so Tain speaks up: "Ah, just shadows, nothin' there."

As they go further, the scene gets a little sunnier. By now the sun is setting, and the kids are looking for a good campsite. Just then, the boat rocks a little, then stops.

"What was that?" Sneezer looks over the side of the boat to see what is there. The water starts to churn and is glowing around them as the boat rocks again.

"Let's row!" Whippy hollers.

Before they can get their oars into the water, the boat nearly flips forward, then slams back down. The kids fall all over the deck, get back up, and row like never before. The smaller boat behind isn't affected as much. As they row out of the churning, bubbling water, the glow disappears and the water is back to normal.

"I don't think whatever it was wanted us here," Ambo says nervously.

Tain looks over at Ambo. "We don't want to be there either, and so we all should be happy."

After a bit, Puff points at the shore. "Well, we seem to be okay now. It's getting late, and I think we're all tired. This is a good place to camp."

They steer the boats toward the shore, where their bows hit the sandy bottom right at the shoreline. The kids grab their gear, get out, and set up camp. They get a fire going, eat their fill, put out the fire, and lay down for the night. They look up through the trees. The sun has now set, and the stars and moon are coming out. The moonlight shines through the trees as their silhouettes add a mystical feel to the starry, moonlit sky. A tiny glow of a fairy can be seen going through the forest now and then. The Neverland night-birds sing their sublime songs once more.

* * * *

The next morning, the Rascals are up early and ready to set sail. They eat a quick breakfast and load the boats. "We can go a little further, but we shouldn't go too far before we head home," says Tain. "The food is getting low already, and Neverfood doesn't seem to work here."

Puff eyes the supplies. "I agree. Let's see what's up around the bend and head home."

The kids all get in the boats and head downstream once again. As they round the bend, they hold their breath in awe. Ahead is a mountain that seems made of precious stones—emeralds, rubies and diamonds mixed with beautiful greenery and turquoise waterfalls. They stop rowing and gaze at the glowing, sparkling sight. "Ooo! Ahhh!"

"How could anything be so beautiful?" Ambo asks, awestruck. As they sit there, drifting down the river, the sunlight reflects off the mountain, making rays of light of every color you can imagine. Some are bright beams; others are shimmering sparkles.

Hawkins, now able to start thinking, speaks up: "We may want to turn around and head home."

Puff looks at her. "We can spend some time here the next time we come back."

They all agree and get the boats going in the opposite direction. One by one they turn around to look again at the unbearable beauty of the mountain. There are no problems this time, and the breeze changes, so they put away the oars and raise the sails, making better time getting back. The sun is setting as they row their boats ashore.

Aky is still in awe of the mountain. "How could anything be so beautiful?"

Puff is back to normal. "We'll find out next time, mate."

"Yes, we will, Puffy." Puff is too tired to care what he is called now.

The Rascals all head for the tree and prepare for Neverfood and bed. It was a great adventure, indeed.

Chapter 86

Barrel of Boys

The next morning's rays wake the Rascals. One by one they head down to the table for breakfast as usual. After eating a big meal and losing their morning faces, they eye each other, looking to the others for ideas for their next plans.

Kilowatts, head in hands, finally speaks: "I think I'm going to rest all day and do nothing."

"Yowsa!" says Okydoky. "That is just wot I aim to be busy at…nuttin'."

With that the kids just laze around, lying on the table or in the grass, some back up in the tree taking a snooze.

* * * *

Aky, laying over one of the barrels, gets an idea. "How about we go to the hill and ride the barrels?"

As all have rested most of the day, the Rascals all agree and head out to what they now call Kite Hill. They drag their barrels up to the top and put some rocks in front of them to keep them from rolling down. Pinner shrugs his shoulders. "Well, who wants to be first?" He points at Ambo, "You up for the barrel ride?"

Ambo shakes her head. "No way am I going to do that!"

Aky raises one hand. "Let me! Let me!"

Whippy looks down the hill, a little unsure. "Okay, if you're up to it."

Aky climbs into the barrel and hollers, "Well, let 'er go!"

Whippy and Kilowatts move the rocks and set Aky's barrel free. It rolls faster and faster, bouncing up and down, finally stopping down by the tree line. Aky emerges but can't stand up, so dizzy from the barrel-roll. Finally getting his feet under him, he says, "Wow, what a ride! Let's go again!"

One by one the kids take a turn until it is Okydoky's turn. He stuffs himself in and throws out his hat. "No room for that thar hat."

The kids let him go. Just like the others, the barrel rolls faster and faster, but this time it heads for a big rock. Sneezer sees this and jumps in front of the barrel to stop it.

"No, Sneezer!" shouts Big C from the top of the hill, but too late. The barrel hits Sneezer, his arms shoot straight up, and it lands on his stomach. He crumples, bent over the barrel, which rolls right over his feet and legs and over the top of him. It then rolls all the way down to the tree line and hits a tree, smashing to smithereens.

Okydoky and Sneezer lie still on the ground for a while, then start to move at the same time, each holding his head and not yet standing up. Oky finally speaks. "That there was some ride. I hit a bump up thar on the hill."

Sneezer looks down at Oky. "That thar bump was me!"

Both are okay, and the kids yell out, "BANGARANG!"

"Another great adventure!" Tain proclaims.

It is getting late, and all the kids start running for the tree while Oky and Sneezer limp in that direction, still recovering from the impact of the runaway barrel.

The adventures in Neverland never seem to end.

Chapter 87

Sad Days at Greystone

Thomas is now getting very old and has been working for another orphanage since Hillshire was closed down and boarded up. He accepted the custodian job at Greystone, because some of the children from Hillshire were transferred there, and it was the only job available; few orphanages are left now.

At Greystone, however, things are much different. The children are not properly cared for, and their conditions are less than adequate. Food and clothing are earned and rarely given. Frequently they are parsed out to jobs in the town without much food, but are expected to work ten hours a day to earn their keep. The children are not only subject to malnutrition, but also to very little education, and sometimes beatings if they refuse to work or ask too many questions. The kids here are often angry and display aggressive behavior because they are mistreated and subject to forced labor, to the benefit of the owners, who are in this business more for the money than the care of the children.

The social services department inspectors are totally unaware of the living conditions or the labor. Whenever inspection time rolls around, the owners give each child a new blanket, pillow, towel, bar of soap and washcloth and then instruct them to smile, be polite to the inspectors, and tell them what a "wonderful place" this is. They are threatened with severe consequences, up to and including ejection into the streets, if they don't go along with the charade.

All of the Hillshire kids are long gone, and Thomas wishes he could now leave. He surely wishes he could help boost the morale of the children at Greystone. He has tried to give them hope by sharing stories of a better time, often referring to Tain, Ambo and the other children he knew and cared for at Hillshire.

Sadly, the children who have been at Greystone for a long time don't believe any of Thomas's stories and often make fun of him. He can't figure out how to reach them, but most heartbreaking for Thomas is when, on particularly difficult days, they harass and badger Koa and Kado, making them cry.

Koa is seven; Kado is six. They are the only ones Thomas can reach. They love it when Thomas secretly tells them the stories of Peter Pan and how Tinker Bell saved the kids from the cold streets. The owners have warned Thomas not to tell the children that there were better days or that they can change their situations: "No stories, no happier times." For they don't want the children to know that things are much better at other institutions. They want them to think this is one of the best places in all of England. Still, Thomas shares the story of the very last day at Hillshire Orphanage, when the children, left behind in the streets, flew away with Tinker Bell in a beautiful cloud of fairy dust.

Now, at six and seven, Kado and Koa know all of the stories by heart. They sigh and dream about Tinker Bell and the cloud of fairy dust, wishing they could go to Neverland. Thomas has told them, "Stay strong, because you never know what could happen. Tinker Bell could show up at any time and take you back with her."

This lifts their spirits each time they hear it.

Chapter 88

Tinker Bell's Big Heart and Big Rescue

Meanwhile, Tain and Ambo are by the treehouse, practicing their sword-fighting, back-and-forth, up on the table and down. When they take a break, Tain says to Ambo, "You were always better than the others."

"Just comes easy for me for some reason." Ambo shrugs her shoulders.

Tain looks over at Ambo and slowly reaches for his sword. Ambo sees him out of the corner of her eye just as he jumps up with his weapon. He shouts, "Except for me!"

Ready for Tain's maneuvers again, they fence it out. After a while, they pause and take a big breath. "I've had enough," Ambo pants.

"Me, too. Whew."

Though it has become harder and harder to remember, Tain reminisces back to the time before they came to Neverland. Looking a little sad, he glances over at Ambo, sitting on top of the table with her legs crossed.

"You know, Ambo, I sure miss Thomas. He was such a good friend."

"Wow, I was just thinking of him, too. How sad it is that he can't be here. He's all alone back there, and it's been so long."

Just then, Pinner walks up to them. "Who is all alone?"

Ambo looks over at Pinner. "We were just talking about Thomas and how sad it is that he can't be here."

Pinner looks down. "We all miss Thomas. He taught us so much, like sword-fighting, fixing and building in the orphanage."

"Yeah," agrees Tain, "we wouldn't have fixed or added to the treehouse, or even built our boats, if it wasn't for what Thomas taught us."

Ambo sheaths her sword and walks away. "How sad."

Tain and Pinner do the same. As they get further away, Tinker Bell flies down from up on a tree limb. She has observed and heard everything. She watches the kids disappear, with one eyebrow up and hands on her hips in a stern stance. "I think it is time for another great adventure. It's time to grab the bag and THT."

She flies off and disappears into the sky with a flash of rainbow colors.

Chapter 89

To Thomas's House

Thomas is in his home, trying to keep warm, burning the remainder of his firewood he gathered the day before. Firewood is not easy to come by in the city. He lives in a one-room shack in a bad part of town. Since he lost his job at the Hillshire orphanage he has struggled to make ends meet and have enough to eat. His pay at Greystone is very little. Some days he goes without a meal.

Thomas uses up his last piece of firewood and eats what is almost the last of his beans and bread. He kneels by his bed to say a prayer and climbs in. With only one cover on the bed, he keeps his clothes on to help keep warm. A stray cat he named Shires has become his only friend and curls up at his feet.

Just before morning, Thomas is startled awake by a bright glow in the room. The cat, awake as well, gives a loud hiss. Just as quickly, Shires relaxes and starts to purr. Multiple colors and silvery sparkles fill the room. Startling Thomas again, Tinker Bell flies down and hovers in front of him. He can't believe his eyes as he remembers when the kids flew away with Tinker Bell. Just like then, he puts his hand on his heart and says quietly, "Is it really you? Are you real?"

Tinker Bell looks up and sighs. "Here we go again. Yes, I am really real. Are you?"

"Hello," says Thomas, not knowing what else to say.

Tinker Bell is anxious to get going. "I overheard the Neverland Rascals saying how much they miss you, so I'm giving them a surprise."

"That's nice… Who are the Neverland Rascals?"

"Oh, yeah, you don't know the kids' new name. Your kids."

"Ohh…my kids… My kids? I don't have kids."

"The kids from the orphanage!"

"Oh…of course, my kids. Why didn't you say so?"

"I did, I… Never mind."

Thomas is growing excited. "How are they? I sure miss them."

Tinker Bell smirks and puts her hand on her chin. "They are doing bangarang."

"What is banga—er, whatever?"

Tinker Bell takes a big breath. "Never mind."

"That is just great, but why are you here? I am glad to meet you, though." He holds his hand out to shake hands with Tinker Bell, then realizes she is too small and quickly pulls it back.

Tinker Bell turns her back to Thomas for a moment. "I am here to give the kids a great surprise."

"Wow, that is great, Tinker Bell… Wait… You are here, and they are there."

She quickly spins around and points at him. "You are the surprise."

He is more confused than ever. "Huh? I am surprised I am the surprise—I think."

She hovers closer to his nose and pokes him in it. "How would you like to go to Neverland and live with the Neverland Rascals?"

Thomas puts his hand on his heart and sits on the edge of the bed. "Oh, my—you mean I could go to Neverland?"

Tinker Bell opens her arms wide. "Yes."

Thomas is almost in a trance. "Oh, my… We fly with fairy dust and all?"

With one hand on her hip she drops a small amount of fairy dust from her fingertips. "Yes, indeed. What will it be? Yes or no?"

He looks around and then back at Tinker Bell. He then stands up. "I have nothing and no one to leave behind. I own nothing. Let's go."

She showers him with fairy dust and says, "Just remember THT."

Thomas is a little nervous, thinking he should know what THT is. "Okay… What is THT?"

"That means Think Happy Thoughts."

"That's an easy one for me. I'm going to Neverland!" His feet leave the ground, and he flies and keeps his balance pretty well for the first time. With all the silvery sparkles and colors filling the room, his voice is a little shaky from excitement. "This has got to be a dream, but…let's go."

Just as quickly, he stops and says, "Wait, I forgot my best friend. Can she go?"

Tinker Bell raises her arms. "We can't take the whole world, you know."

Thomas points to the cat sitting on the edge of the bed, looking anxious. Tinker Bell puts her hand on her chin in contemplation. "Hmmm…well, okay, but no one else." She sprinkles Shires with fairy dust, and the cat starts to rise. He freaks out and claws frantically at the air. Thomas and Tinker Bell laugh at the sight. He flies over, grabs the cat, and holds her close.

Tinker Bell points to the window. "We are off!" Out the window they all fly, Tinker Bell in the lead.

Chapter 90

The Koa and Kado Rescue

Before they get too far, Thomas stops Tinker Bell. "Wait. There's just one more thing."

Tinker Bell is a little frustrated. "Now what?"

Thomas speaks low. "I can't leave without my other two kids at the orphanage. They are only six and seven, but they believe in you and Neverland. The only ones. It would break their heart if I never came back for them."

Tinker Bell puts her hand on her chin again. "Well, I told you we can't take the whole world—"

Thomas interrupts with his head down. "I know, but they believe in you, and I always tell them you could come back at any time and rescue them."

"Why doesn't anyone let me finish? As I was saying, I can't take the whole world, but since they are only six and seven"—pointing at Thomas—"let's get 'em."

Thomas does a backflip in the air. "This way."

Thomas, Tinker Bell, and Shires finally arrive at the orphanage, where Thomas opens the second-story window and flies in. Landing on the floor, he walks to the big room where many of the orphans are sleeping. He opens the door and quietly walks over to Koa and Kado's beds. While waking them up, he tries to keep them quiet, not wanting to explain what is about to happen. So they follow Thomas, half-asleep in their long white nightgowns, not knowing what is going on. They walk down the hallway to the open window, where Thomas stands them up on the windowsill.

"What are you doing?" says Koa, scared. "It is a long way down."

"Don't worry, Koa. You will be flying shortly. Remember what I told you about Tinker Bell?"

"Yeah."

"Well, here she is."

Tinker Bell flies down right in front of Koa and Kado. They jump and fall back to the floor, but Thomas catches them. Kado reaches out to Tinker Bell. "You are really real."

"You are the first to get it," she says, pointing at Kado.

"Tinker Bell, meet Koa and Kado," says Thomas. "Brother and sister."

Just then, the door to the kids' bedroom burst open, and the other kids, who never believed Thomas, storm out running toward him. One of the kids who always gave Thomas a bad time says, "What are you doing by the open window with Koa and Kado? You pushing them out or something?"

"You never believed me," Thomas says, "but look at this!"

Tinker Bell sprinkles Koa and Kado with fairy dust, and they start to float away. Another kid speaks up. "I want to go, too."

Thomas shakes his head. "Shouldn't have doubted me and treated me mean."

Tinker Bell leads Thomas, Shires, Koa and Kado out the window. The other kids run to the window and watch with their mouths open as the five disappear. Tinker Bell's colorful, sparkling glow slowly fades into the starry sky as the sun's glow on the horizon peeks through.

Chapter 91

"Y'all Sho' am One Good Fairy"

In Neverland, the kids go about their usual activities—looking for great adventures they make up, or just lazing around under the big tree. As the day goes by and the moon starts to rise, Whippy says, "You know, I haven't seen Tinker Bell all day."

"I all haven't seen her none, neither," says Okydoky in his southern drawl.

As they are talking, they don't notice the flash of rainbow colors as Tinker Bell, Thomas, Shires, Koa and Kado enter Neverland. They land a ways away in the sand, high on the cliffs. Tinker Bell helps Thomas as they land, since he is older and has not yet felt Neverland's effects. He hits the sand, falls to his knees, and lets Shires go. Shires again paws frantically in the air but gently sets down and digs into the sand with all four feet. He looks up with a cat-frown as Koa and Kado hit the sand feet-first and fall into it face-first, as newcomers do.

Thomas is stunned by the beauty and colors he has never seen before. Shires, amazed as well, lets out a "Meeeooo-wow."

Thomas looks at Shires and back at Tinker Bell. "Did I just hear what I heard?"

Tinker Bell laughs. "This is Neverland! Koa and Kado, you follow Thomas."

He can hardly contain himself. He is actually in Neverland, a true-life fairy tale. "Let's go surprise…the Neverland Rascals," he says excitedly.

Tinker Bell is just as enthusiastic. "Let me go first, then you come from behind the big tree when I motion for you."

* * * *

Tinker Bell flies over to the table. "I'm starved. Let's eat."

"We are eating!" Aky blurts. "Where have you been?"

Tinker Bell gave a little chuckle. "Oh, on a great adventure."

Ambo is curious. "What kind of adventure, Tinker Bell?"

"A surprise adventure."

"What kind of adventure is that?" Crane asks, throwing his hands up.

"I have with me someone you may know."

Big C points in the air. "There is no one with you. What kinda game are you playing?"

Tinker Bell pauses. "A Thomas game."

"No such game," says Sneezer.

Tinker Bell motions for Thomas to come from behind the tree, but out comes Shires. Big C looks at Tinker Bell, puzzled. "A cat is our surprise? Nice kitty, though."

"Meet Thomas, Koa, Kado, and Shires."

Out the rest come. The kids gasp and can't believe their eyes. There is a moment of silence, and then a roar: "Thomas! Thomas!" They holler as they rush toward their old friend. They hug him so much they almost knock him down. Some cry with happy tears.

After a long while they all sit down. "I overheard Ambo and Tain talking about Thomas and how they missed him," Tinker Bell says. "That is when I decided to go after him."

"Tinker Bell, y'all sho' am one good fairy," Okydoky says. "Yessum, yo sho' am."

Hawkins points to Koa and Kado. "And someone just my size."

All the kids thank Tinker Bell as the night sky darkens, the moon brightens in the starry sky, and they all get ready for bed. Hawkins, so excited, says to Ambo, "I don't know if I can sleep. I am so happy."

Ambo looks over at Hawkins with a tear in her eye. "So happy, Hawkins… so happy."

The moon and the stars create an aurora effect in the night sky, punctuated by the glow of fairies flitting here and there as the night-birds sing. Mystical trees tower high, and flowers glow below. Living in Neverland is just like a dream.

The End . . .

of the Beginning

Look up to a ceiling of stars.

Adventures there are farther than far

Beyond the beyond and shooting stars.

The brightest star to the right,

You'll go back, in your dreams at night.

You laugh and crow under starlight.

The Neverland Rascals Theme Song

BY TED SNYDER

We are the Neverland Rascals,

We laugh, joke, and sing.

We are the Neverland Rascals,

Capable of anything.

We are the Neverland Rascals,

We come and go as we please.

We are the Neverland Rascals

From the mountains to the seas.

Far beyond the moon

We never clean our room.

Neverland is our playroom,

And we always sing a tune,

Like ...

We are the Neverland Rascals,

We'll never have to wash up.

We are the Neverland Rascals,

We'll never ever grow up.

We are the Neverland Rascals,

Always having fun.

We are the Neverland Rascals,

Got pirates on the run.

We are happy, happier,

Happiest, happieriest

Delighted, contented,

Lucky, merry, and free…

That's what we am,

That's what we be.

Characters

Puff: 12 years old. Reddish-blonde, big puffy hair. Likes to be in charge.

Crane: 12 years old. Tall and thin, with large hooked nose. Light brown hair, normal length. A little loud when he speaks.

Sneezer: 8 years old. Scruffy and dirty with messed-up light brown hair. Always sneezing.

PJ's: 8 years old. Reddish hair, normal length. Likes magic tricks.

Big C: 10 years old. Considered the intellectual. Thick black-rimmed glasses. Dark hair combed straight down. Sometimes causes accidents, but never on purpose.

Kilowatts: 10 years old. A little heavy, and always looking for food. Bright short red hair, sticks straight out.

Hawkins: 7 years old. A small, tough girl with reddish blond hair. When she gets angry, she says, "I'll rip your lip!" When angry she also doubles her fists with arms straight down and leans forward with her chin out and a big frown.

Aky: 12 years old. Always looking for a way to get a thrill. Adrenalin junky. Tall, thin with brown hair.

Ambo: 12 years old. Strong, smart, good-looking girl with dishwater-blond hair. Always beating the boys at games and sword-fighting. Good attitude.

Tain: 12 years old. Always happy, fast to smile. Considerate of others. Athletic and brave. Likes to help out.

Whippy: 11 years old. Likes to be in charge, like Puff. Short, dishwater-blond hair. A little heavy and very animated. Wears a captain's hat.

Okydoky: 10 years old. Very short sandy-blonde hair, strong southern drawl, wears bib overalls cut off at the knees, no shirt, straw hat, and usually chews a piece of straw. Slow movements and speech.

Pinner: 10 years old. Very skinny. Some say he is so skinny his feet could stick in solid rock.

Thomas: Starts out younger but is very old by the end of the story. His job is maintenance at the orphanages. Loves the kids. Teaches them sword-fighting, carpentry, and taking care of buildings. Tells stories of Peter Pan to the kids.

Koa: 7 years old. Brother to Kado. Sandy-blond hair. Lives at the Greystone orphanage.

Kado: 6 years old. Sister to Koa. Sandy-blond hair. Lives at the Greystone orphanage.

Jenks: One of Hook's pirates. Very clumsy. Unibrow and large, snaggly buck teeth.

Sparky: Another of Hook's pirates. Heavy and wrinkly hound-dog sad face. Doesn't speak much. Friend of Jenks.

Tootles: Original Lost Boy, but much older.

Peter Pan: Grown up until he goes back to Neverland. Has a family.

Tricia: Peter's wife. Very matter-of-fact and practical.

Amber: Peter's daughter. Helpful and friendly.

Clint: Peter's son. Can be impatient and mischievous, but also helpful.

Poppy: Wendy's friend. Short and a little stocky, with blond curly hair and excitable.

Goatee: A white goat with small horns curved back. Goes crazy whenever someone sneezes

Bangarangatang: A spider monkey with very crooked popping eyes. Friendly with the kids.

Captain Hook: Leader of the pirates. Peter Pan cut off his hand in a swordfight long ago, so he wears a hook in its place and has vowed vengeance on Peter ever since.

Smee: Hook's close chubby pirate friend. Not like Hook at all.

Various Pirates.

Tinkerbell: A fairy that helps take care of the kids in Neverland. Fiery attitude and red hair. Very strong and fast.

THINK HAPPY THOUGHTS!